A Taste Of Magick

BARBARA DEVLIN

This is a work of fiction. Names, characters, organizations, places, events, and incidents are either products of the author's imagination or are used fictitiously.

A Taste of Magick Copyright © 2017 Barbara Devlin

All rights reserved.

No part of this book may be reproduced, or stored in a retrieval system, or transmitted in any form or by any means, electronic, mechanical, photocopying, recording or otherwise, without the express written permission of the publisher.

Published by Barbara Devlin

Cover art by Dar Albert

ISBN: 978-1-945576-84-3

DEDICATION

For those who embrace the magick in their lives.

CONTENTS

Prologue	1
Chapter One	7
Chapter Two	30
Chapter Three	50
Chapter Four	70
Chapter Five	90
Chapter Six	111
Epilogue	128

PROLOGUE

June, 2014

"*Class of twenty-fourteen* rules!"
"Seniors kick ass!"

The shouts jolted Russell Lee McBride alert, as he zipped his jeans and raked his fingers through his hair. Sitting in the backseat of his Camaro, which he parked beneath the large canopy of a tree behind the Old Haven Mill tavern, a business he inherited with his sister, he glanced at Cindy Parker, as she pulled down her skirt and buttoned her blouse.

"You all right? And why didn't you tell me it was your first time?" Not that he would've changed his mind about the pretty waitress from the tavern, because he'd always wanted a piece of her tight ass, and now he'd had her, as a graduation present to himself. "I'd have gone easier on you."

Well, probably not.

"It wasn't that bad." Even in the dark, her overwhelming vulnerability blanketed him in emotions he couldn't contain, because he'd never admitted the truth about his so-called gift, so he didn't know how to manage it. No one—not even his parents, when they were alive, knew of his power. "Really, I'm okay, and you didn't force me."

"I know." As guilt set in, he shifted his weight, reached forward, and opened the door. "I just wish I'd known."

"Don't worry about it," she said, as he stepped from the car. "I'm all right."

But her vibe said something else, and he couldn't shake it.

Like his older sister, Mary-George, Russ had been born into a family with a history of magick, in a small town infested with witches, the real kind, because they existed, and to his disgust, he'd been cursed with the claircognizance of desire, or what his sister called a gut hunch. In short, he knew what people wanted, and he knew that cute little Cindy wanted him, so he took advantage of her in a moment of weakness and popped her cherry.

"We need to get moving." Outside, he stretched tall, turned, and grabbed her by the wrist. "Come on, before the guys find us."

As the star football player for the Ospreys of Haven Harbor High School, Russ had a reputation to consider. While boning the poor girl half the team chased would win him some serious points, he didn't want to hurt her, because she was nice to him. She was genuine, as opposed to those other chicks that looked at him as another notch in their bedpost. Although she'd never said anything, she cared about him.

And he just wanted to fuck her.

Then again, he had a wicked crush on Cindy, but his buddies wouldn't get that. They didn't get a lot of things.

In the distance, fire burned in a barrel, and his friends danced and goofed off in a circle, as they drank beer they stole from the local store. During the day, the woods behind the tavern belonged to Mary-George, and she spent hours hiking the trails. At night, the cool kids ruled, and Russ was the king.

"I've never been to one of the wild parties." Clutching his arm, she smiled, and excitement poured from her. "And I never would've imagined going with the most popular guy in school."

"Yeah, about that." He pulled free and rubbed the back of his neck. "Look, it's mainly my crew, and you'd be bored, so why don't you go home?"

"You don't want to be seen with me?" The pain in her tone cut through him like a knife, and it pissed him off, because he didn't want any trouble. "Are you ashamed of me? Are you afraid of what your friends will think?"

"Hey, it's not like that." He lied. "I just wanna hang with my buds, okay? And you're not my girlfriend or anything."

Her shoulders slumped. "But, we just—"

"We just—what?" He kicked a rock and swore. "We screwed, big deal, because everybody does it." He shrugged. "I mean, I might have been your first, but I'm betting I won't be your last, so be cool, and I'll call you tomorrow."

"Do you promise?" Shuffling her feet, she pouted.

"Yep." Another lie.

"Okay." Damn, she was disappointed and desperate. "Oh, and I'm on shift at the tavern, at five."

"Got it." As Russ retreated toward the woods, he saluted, and Cindy waved. "Talk to you later."

Blowing out a breath, he followed the well-worn path, winding through the dense brush, until he joined his gang.

"Well, well, it's about time." Jeff waggled his brows. "So, how was she?"

It was sweet, but Russ would never admit that.

"How was who?" From the ice chest, he grabbed a beer, twisted the cap, took a big gulp, and burped. "Let's get this party started."

"Come on, man." Brian bowed. "We're not worthy."

"I don't know what you're talking about, because I got stuck closing the tavern." Russ sat on a fallen log. "Now I just wanna chill."

"Sidney told us she saw you with Cindy, in the back of your car." Tony kissed his cheerleader girlfriend, a stuck-up bitch with a vicious streak Russ couldn't stand. "Dude, I can't believe you bagged the Parker babe, when she turned down our star pitcher, last summer, and that seriously chapped his ass."

"Hell, I've been trying to get in her panties for a year." Tommy raised a bottle in toast. "My man."

"Bet she wears some cheap store brand, because she can't afford lace." Brittney, another mean girl, smirked. "Or is she so poor she goes commando?"

Russ gritted his teeth, before he told everyone that Brittney couldn't give decent head.

"Does she give as good as she gets?" Thrusting his hips in a crude rhythm, Shane laughed. "Cut it up with us."

"Hey, I don't kiss and tell." Then, for some reason, Russ grinned. "But Cindy Parker knows how to peel a banana."

"*I knew it.*" Larry slapped his thighs, and everyone burst into laughter.

It was then the clouds parted, and moonlight bathed the clearing in a silver veil. To the hoots and howls of his buddies, Russ skipped in a circle—until he spotted Cindy crouched in the trees."

CHAPTER ONE

October, 2017

Regret festered, seeped into the soul, and poisoned life. Infecting each successive interaction, contaminating every relationship, and spoiling rare moments of happiness, remorse only intensified in the three years since Russell departed home, leaving nothing untouched by guilt. No matter how far or fast he ran, he couldn't escape the pain that followed him everywhere, so he decided to stop running. That was why he left school in Boston, to return to Haven Harbor.

Because he had to make things right with Cindy Parker.

As he turned onto Raven Road, he tightened his grip on the steering wheel of his old Camaro and tried not to think of what happened in the backseat, but that fateful night was never far from his mind. He tried to sell his muscle car, once, but he couldn't go through with it, because he needed the reminder, like an albatross around his neck, of what he did to someone he cared about, although he never told her the truth.

When he spotted the quirky house with the flock of plastic pink flamingos in the front yard, he shook his head. As he pulled into the driveway, Granny Minnie rushed to greet him.

"There's my boy." Reeking of mentholated rub, which always made him think of her, she gave him a hug and a big kiss on the cheek. "I've got dinner almost ready, and your room is just how you like it."

"Thanks, granny." From the trunk, he pulled two suitcases. "And I appreciate you taking me in on short notice."

"Well, I'm happy to have you." She climbed the stairs and held open the screened door. "But I don't understand why you couldn't stay with Mary-George, as you have since you started them fancy college classes."

"Without getting too graphic, there's no privacy at her place, now that Rafe has moved in with her." In the modest living room, which featured furniture still covered in

A TASTE OF MAGICK

cellophane packing wrap, a framed, velvet picture of Elvis over the fireplace, and a *Miami Vice* poster on the wall, Russ set his things on the pink shag carpet. "The last time I was there, I couldn't get any sleep. And I know they're adults, and now they're engaged, but it's weird, because George is my sister. I don't want to think about, much less hear, her having sex."

"Fair enough." Granny cackled and narrowed her stare when some sort of timer rang in the kitchen. "That'll be my roast. Do me a favor and run over to the Parkers and invite that sweet little Cindy to eat with us. Tell her I won't take no for an answer. You know her mother passed away, in March."

In that moment, Minnie could've knocked him over with a feather, because he wasn't expecting to see Cindy so soon. Hell, he needed to drink plenty of liquid courage before facing her.

"Okay." Of course, that was easier said than done. "And I'd heard the news from George."

"Well, get a move on, because I'm so hungry I could eat my toenails."

"Yes, ma'am." After carrying his suitcases to his room, he combed his hair and rubbed his stubbly chin. Sifting through his things, he located his electric shaver, walked to the bathroom, and gave himself a quick cleanup.

By the time he stepped outside, the sun sat low on the horizon, and a cold breeze sliced through his button-down shirt. Fortunately, Cindy lived only two doors down from Minnie, so he didn't have far to go.

The Craftsman-style home looked brand new, with a fresh coat of paint in complimenting green and brown colors, and clusters of yellow mums in large terracotta pots sat at either side of the entry.

As he skipped up the porch stairs, he noted the same old ten-speed bike, with a dented purple frame, which she used to ride to school, propped against the rail. As he was about to knock, Cindy appeared behind the screened door, and the emotions she projected when she recognized him almost brought him to his knees.

"Russell Lee, is that you?" Considering the pain she broadcast, she knew damn well it was him. "What are you doing here?"

"Minnie wants you to join us for dinner, and she said she won't take no for an answer." God, Cindy was beautiful. Still long and lean, with thick blonde hair and blue eyes, she hadn't changed a bit since they graduated high school. "I know it's not the nicest invitation, but you know my granny."

"Yes, I do." She waved, as if nothing was wrong, as though he hadn't crushed her, but the anguish she cast declared otherwise. She didn't want him there, and he didn't blame her. "Come inside, while I grab a sweater and change my shoes, because I just finished a shift at the tavern, and I don't want to dirty Minnie's pink carpet."

"Yeah, she's pretty proud of it." To his surprise, polished wood and leather furniture, with stained and varnished wainscoting, decorated the living room, and a huge flat-screen television hung over the hearth. "I'm sorry about your mom."

"Me, too," Cindy called from her bedroom. "But I'm glad she's finally at peace and no longer suffering, because it was rough in the end."

"Cancer, right?" In the dining area, Russell discovered a nice oak table and a desk tucked in the corner, with a computer and stacks of papers. "You attending classes at UMass?"

"What?" With her locks in a ponytail, she looked about fifteen, as she caught him snooping around her things. "Oh, that? I'm taking online courses."

"What are you studying?" Impressed, he gazed at her and smiled like a lovesick idiot, because his crush resurfaced with a vengeance. "And when do you find the time, because I thought my sister kept you pretty busy?"

"Accounting." Leaning against the wall, she folded her arms. "And I set my alarm early in the morning, so I can study and complete assignments before I report to the tavern."

"What do you want to do with your degree?" With newfound respect, he admired her dedication, because she'd had it tough as a kid, yet she was doing better than most of his classmates. "Planning to leave Haven Harbor? Is that why you fixed up the place? You gonna flip it?"

"I came into some money from mom's life insurance. It wasn't much, but it paid her medical and funeral bills, paid off the mortgage, and left me with some extra cash." Cindy shrugged. "I put some toward the house, because this is my home, and I'm not going anywhere, so I redid the kitchen and the bathroom, installed a new roof, and put the rest in the bank." Picking up her purse, she motioned with her head. "Come on, before Minnie goes on the war path and comes looking for us, because then we'll both be in trouble."

A TASTE OF MAGICK

"You know her well." Russ laughed, but it did little to dispel the tension between them. He needed to apologize, but it didn't feel right. Then again, would there ever be a right time to apologize for what he did to her?

"Your grandmother seems to think I'm one of her charges, because she feeds me, regularly." On the porch, she held the door for him. Once he crossed the threshold, she locked the bolt. "But it's nice to have company, sometimes."

"So you're not dating anyone?" Searing agony bored through his stomach, because she wanted him gone, and he could've kicked himself for asking that question.

"No, there's no one." Still, she kept her poise. "Between shifts at the tavern and my studies, there aren't enough hours in the day."

"I know what you mean." Kicking a pebble, he tried to play it cool. "Now that George is planning a wedding, I'm gonna have my hands full with the tavern."

"You're coming back to work?" Palpable shock rocked him, as Cindy stopped in her tracks. "You're moving back to Haven Harbor?"

"Yeah." Embarrassed, because he knew, without a doubt, that he caused her so much pain, he shuffled his feet. "Boston is great, but it's not for me, because Haven Harbor is my home. Guess you and I have that in common, and now we're neighbors."

"You're staying with Minnie?" she asked, as they returned to Granny's house.

"He sure is, and he'd better have a darned good excuse for making me wait to eat." With fists on hips, Granny Minnie stood in the doorway to the kitchen. "What took you so long? I could've run to the hospital and back, by now, and I'm starved. Now, wash your hands and get to the table."

"Yes, ma'am." Russ glanced at Cindy and rolled his eyes. "She hasn't changed, a bit. I always figured she'd mellow with age, but I think we'll have to bury her with a treadmill."

"I heard that," Minnie replied.

"Shh." Cindy laughed. "Trust me, you don't want to incur her wrath, and something smells delicious."

"Aw, aren't you sweet, Miss Parker." Minnie preened, as they cleaned up at the sink. "But you're still too skinny, and I'm gonna fatten you up, if it's the last thing I do."

"Hey, you've made a good start, because I'm having trouble fitting into my favorite jeans." Cindy looked damn good to him, as she passed him the towel. "Is there anything I can do to help you, Minnie?"

"Nope." Lifting her chin, as she carried a platter to the table, granny grinned. "Just take a seat and prepare to be amazed."

"You're too modest, Granny." When Russ pulled out a chair for Cindy, she took the opposite seat. "But, damn, I missed your cooking."

"Watch your language in the presence of a lady, young man, or I'll wash your mouth out with soap." Shaking a wooden spoon, Granny frowned. Then she dished big portions of pot roast, with large chunks of potatoes and carrots. "Why don't you do something useful and try one of those rolls?"

"You don't have to ask me twice." He pulled a beauty from the breadbasket, slathered butter across the top, and took a bite. "Mmm, this is incredible."

"You can thank Cindy for that." Granny sat and pulled a napkin into her lap. "Bought 'em fresh this morning."

"Oh, yeah?" When he stared at his former classmate, she blushed. "I didn't know you cooked."

"Ever since Reese Maxwell contracted with several hotels in Boston, he closed the Old-Fashioned Grist Mill and Bakery to the public, and I filled in the gap." Cindy toyed with a carrot on her plate, and he sensed desire. She wanted something—something important to her, yet she seemed unsure of herself. Then and there, Russ vowed to find out what that was and help her get it, because he owed her that. He owed her a lot. "I bake a selection of items, every morning, before the tavern opens for business, and sell them out of the gift shop, with your sister's permission."

"Mary-George thinks you should open a bakery, in town." Granny nodded to Russ, and he realized, to his horror, she played matchmaker. "And I agree, because you're almost as skilled in the kitchen, as me. By the way, I made a bowl of my famous cucumber salad, just for you. Don't forget it when you leave."

"Oh, Minnie, what am I going to do with you?" Cindy shook her head. "But I can't complain, because I love your cucumber salad. In fact, I make a batch of your signature recipe, every week, for myself."

"Then I've saved you the trouble, haven't I," Minnie crowed.

"Yes, ma'am." Cindy shifted, and beneath the table, her foot briefly touched his, and she flinched.

The rest of the meal passed in relative silence, even when Minnie brought in her award-winning Perilously Perverted Peach

Cobbler Plague, which most folks simply called, 'The Plague.'

All too soon, Cindy stood and pulled on her sweater, to leave, when Russ just wanted her to stay.

"Thanks, for dinner, Minnie." Cindy stacked the dirty plates and carried them to the sink. "I can help wash dishes, and then I need to get home, because five o'clock comes early, and I've had a long day."

"Don't you worry about that. Russell Lee's not allergic to soap and water, and I'll put him to work after he walks you home." From the refrigerator, Granny retrieved a pile of plastic containers. "There's some of my pot roast, the cucumber salad, and the plague, and don't you waste none of it."

"I won't, I promise. And I appreciate the food, more than you know, Minnie." Resting her chin atop the pile, Cindy balanced the collection. "And I know the way home, so I don't need an escort."

"But it's dark out." Russ picked up his jacket and followed her.

"I'm a big girl, and I can take care of myself." With a thrust of her hip, Cindy opened the screened door. "Goodnight."

As if on guard, Granny stood on the porch with him, until Cindy skipped up the stairs of her house, and then they returned to the living room.

After shutting and locking the door, Minnie turned to Russ and narrowed her stare. "What did you do to the Parker girl?"

~

The streets of Haven Harbor were quiet, and most of the windows were dark, as Cindy rode her bike through town, on her way to work. Light rain made the journey slow going, and fierce winds left her squinting and shivering. By the time she rolled into the parking lot, she was frozen clean through to her undies.

As usual, the beat up, green Chevy Vega sat near the loading dock, and she called a greeting to Tony, the tavern cook, as she pulled her bike inside the break room and hung her raincoat on a peg. After punching her time card, she donned a hairnet and an apron.

"Morning, Cindy." Looming over a steaming pot, he waved. "We've had five calls to reserve a loaf of your herbed bread, Lometa Adams will be here to pick up Josiah's birthday cake at three, and the chef at The Judges Chambers wants to know if you've got time to bake four dozen dinner rolls." The cook snickered. "Girl, you're the hottest ticket in town, but I'm not complaining, because my to-go orders doubled with your business. I told Mary-George we should consider expanding into catering."

"I'm on it." As she darted about the kitchen, she collected the necessary ingredients and deposited them on the massive stainless steel counter. From the refrigerator, she pulled the two layers of cake she'd baked last night. "And I think you're crazy. Wait—I know you're crazy, because we can barely keep up with demand."

"Then it's a good thing we've got an extra pair of hands." To her horror, Russell Lee walked into the kitchen.

Dressed in jeans and a tavern t-shirt, the short sleeves of which accentuated his muscled arms, and his thick brown hair neatly combed, he looked way too beautiful at that hour. Of course, she'd always thought he was gorgeous.

The problem was he knew it.

To her embarrassment, she'd let that pretty façade fool her into believing he was a nice guy, when the truth was he was ugly on the inside. For the rest of her life, she'd regret what she did on graduation night.

"Hey, boss two, how you doing?" Tony

peered over his shoulder. "Can't believe you beat your sister, but I think George is running late, because she's usually here, by now."

"Did someone say my name?" Bringing up the rear, Mary-George walked in and went straight to work, tugging a skillet from the overhead rack. "I'm dragging, today, and I don't know why."

"I know the reason." Tony snorted. "Too much bouncy bounce with that fiancé of yours, although I'm glad he finally decided to make an honest woman out of you, when I'd long ago given up hope."

"Aw, that's sweet, but you shouldn't have concerned yourself." Mary-George inclined her head and smiled. "Because you're proof positive that for every squirrel there's a nut."

The pointed but friendly spirit that characterized the tavern staff was the main reason Cindy remained at the restaurant, after what happened with Russell Lee. While they weren't related, her fellow servers were family. After her mom died, Mary-George, Tony, and the other waiters, along with Minnie Terwilliger, were all Cindy had in the world, and she wasn't about to give them up because some jerk disappointed her.

"What do you want me to do, sis?" Russ donned an apron. "I'd go to the office, but it looks like I'm needed, here."

"Why don't you help Cindy with the girly stuff?" While Tony was just being Tony, his offhand suggestion put her in a difficult position, but he couldn't have known that.

Yet, in silence she screamed.

"Sure thing." Cool and calm, as if nothing had ever happened between them, with a boyish grin that once melted her heart but no longer swayed her, Russ strolled to her side. "What can I do for you?"

Drop dead.

Of course, the minute she formed the thought she regretted it.

That was the worst part of remorse—the never-ending guilt.

In the years since he screwed her and then tossed her aside like yesterday's newspaper, she'd wised up, but she never forgot her first crush, because he remained a very real part of her life.

From the football field of Haven Harbor High School, where she watched the games every season, to the tavern, where they waited tables, to Minnie's house, where they often had dinner as an extended family, of a sort, Russell Lee was everywhere, and she reached for him, despite what he did to her, in the dark recesses of her mind. He'd been her hero, and when such fantasies collapsed, they fell a hard, prolonged death. In some respects, they never really disappeared.

For the next four hours, the foursome toiled like a well-oiled machine, putting out delicious home cooking in anticipation of the lunch rush. At every opportunity, she avoided Russ.

In the gift shop, Cindy filled a large display with a variety of cupcakes, tarts, cookies, pastries, pies, loaves of bread, and rolls. Within an hour, most of her inventory was gone, and she had several orders for the next day.

"You know, Tony's right. Although, if you ever tell him I uttered those words I'll fire you." Mary-George scanned the now almost empty cases. "You really should consider opening a bakery, because there's major demand, and you're bringing in a small fortune."

"Between you and me, I want to do it, but I've had no formal training." Cindy glanced left and then right. "I've saved some money, I've picked out a nice little storefront at the corner of Birch and Oak, and I've got an appointment with a loan officer at the Common Ground Savings and Loan. Of course, if it all goes through, I'll give you two weeks' notice."

"You have natural talent, and you'll continue to supply the tavern with your homemade desserts." Mary-George shrieked and pulled Cindy into a bear hug. "Oh, I'm so thrilled for you, and I know you're going to be a huge success."

Swaying, Mary-George stumbled backwards and fainted.

"*Tony.*" Dropping to the floor, Cindy patted Mary-George's cheek. "Tony, come quick. Something's wrong with the boss."

The cook rushed into the gift shop and swore. "What the—call an ambulance."

"What happened?" Russ pushed aside Cindy. "And there's no time for that. Help me get her into my car, and I'll drive to the ER."

"Hurry." Tony scooped Mary-George into his arms. "Cindy, get the door and then call Rafe."

"I don't have his number," she replied.

"I'll call him." From his pocket, Russ fished his cell phone and then unlocked his painfully familiar Camaro. "Put George in the back."

"I'll stay here and take care of the restaurant." After easing Mary-George to the seat, Tony waved at Cindy. "Get in, and make sure the boss doesn't hit her head."

At his command, Cindy feared she might puke.

Shutting out the pain of the past, she eased into the car and cradled Mary-George.

"Rafe said they'd be waiting for us." Russ jumped behind the wheel. "Let's go."

As they sped from the parking lot and veered onto Mill Street, she gazed out the window and tried to breathe, but the memories of that night, three years ago, came back to her in vivid detail.

"Are you all right?" he asked—just like he did after he took her virginity and destroyed her faith.

"I'm fine." Of course, she wasn't fine. She'd never be fine. "Please, hurry."

The stretch of River Road seemed endless, as he drove toward the bluff, where the Haven Harbor Medical Center sat. When they pulled into the ER bay, Rafe and Minnie pushed a stretcher to the curb.

"Let me take her." Rafe brushed aside Cindy and lifted Mary-George, with care. After laying her on the stretcher, he kissed her forehead. "Baby, can you hear me? I'm here, and you're going to be fine."

"What happened?" Minnie took Cindy by the arm, and they walked into the hospital.

A TASTE OF MAGICK

"Was she sick?"

"I don't know." Cindy shrugged. "We were just talking, and she passed out, cold."

"It's okay, child." To Russ and Cindy, Minnie said, "You two wait here, while we get her settled. Once we know something, I'll come get you."

In the waiting room, Russ paced before the windows, while Cindy pretended to read some cheesy gossip magazine, because she didn't want to talk to him, and she couldn't seem to shed the dirty feeling, after riding in the backseat of his car.

After an hour, some young intern came out and stared starry-eyed at Russell Lee. Cindy wanted to warn the girl that he wasn't a nice guy.

"We're pretty slow today, so Nurse Terwilliger said you can come back." The intern smiled. "And Dr. Owen is with Miss McBride."

Stationed at the opening of a curtain, Minnie peered over her shoulder and waved. "Come on, because she's awake and asking for you."

"We're just waiting on some test results," Rafe explained. "But thanks for bringing her in, because I know she'd have refused treatment if she was conscious."

"Yes, I would, because there's nothing wrong with me." Mary-George folded her arms. "Don't see why you're making such a fuss, when I didn't eat breakfast, because my stomach was a little upset, and that's probably why I fainted."

"I told you, so." Rafe arched a brow. "And I made your favorite—scrambled eggs and cinnamon rolls, and it went into the trash."

"I said I was sorry." Mary-George pouted, and Rafe kissed her.

"Well, I think we know the source of your symptoms." Another doctor yanked aside the divider. "Tell me something. How long have you been feeling queasy, in the morning?"

"I dunno." Mary-George shrugged. "For a little while."

"Why didn't you say something?" Rafe huffed a breath.

"Because I knew you'd overreact." She sniffed. "And I'm sure it's nothing."

"Actually, it's something." The physician chuckled and handed Rafe a chart. "I hear you just got engaged to Dr. Owen, so it appears congratulations are in order on two fronts."

"Oh, baby." Rafe laughed, tossed the chart on a bedside table, and framed her face.

"We're pregnant."

"What?" Mary-George's mouth fell agape. "Are you serious?"

As the tender scene played out, and Rafe and Mary-George shared a thorough kiss, Cindy envied her longtime friend, because she'd always dreamed of a loving husband and a family.

"I knew it." Minnie clapped and then hugged Mary-George. "I just knew it."

"You gotta be kidding." Russ chucked Rafe's shoulder. "Don't you suit up when you bang my sister?"

"Hey, watch your mouth." Rafe smacked Russ. "I don't *bang* George, I make love to her. Maybe one day you'll grow up and learn the difference."

"Sorry, Rafe." Russ sobered. "I didn't mean anything by it."

"Well, I guess the wedding is going to happen sooner than later, now that you've knocked up my granddaughter." Minnie cackled. "And I couldn't be happier, because we can arrange it right here, in Haven Harbor. You don't need no fancy New York ceremony, when we've got the community center."

As the focus turned to talk of gowns, cake, and flowers, everything seemed to go hazy.

Cindy retreated and then ran down the hall. She didn't stop until she reached the picnic table that overlooked the sea. Leaning forward, she gasped for air, and her ears pealed, as the world seemed to collapse about her.

"Cindy, are you all right?" The statement came to her as if from afar. As though the teenaged Russell had clawed through space and time to hurt her again.

"Why are you here?" Gritting her teeth, she clenched her fists. "What do you want from me? Haven't you taken enough? Why can't you leave me alone?"

"Because I came home for you."

That was the last thing she expected him to say.

"Why?" To ground herself in reality, she dug her fingernails into her palms. "What am I to you?"

"I'm sorry, Cindy."

"For what?"

"For what I did."

"You can't even say it, can you?"

"No, I can't. But that doesn't mean I don't regret what happened."

"Do you know what I have to put up with, every time one of your friends comes into the tavern?"

A TASTE OF MAGICK

"No, but I think can imagine."

"No, you can't, because they don't call you a slut." She looked him in the eye. "They don't proposition you. They don't threaten to take you behind the tavern and fuck you."

"I'm sorry." He moved toward her, and she retreated. "I'm so sorry."

"Stay away from me." When he rounded the table, she ran in the opposite direction.

"I'm not gonna hurt you." Russ stopped and splayed his palms. "Let me drive you to the tavern or home, if you want."

"No thanks." Cindy backed toward the ER. "I can find my own way, just like I did that night."

CHAPTER TWO

It was late in the evening, when Russ filled the last bag with leaves and scanned Cindy's yard for any rogues. Leaning the rake against the house, he searched for the hose. After watering the pots on the porch, he pulled off his gloves.

"What are you doing?" On the sidewalk, Cindy slowed and slipped off her bike. "Russell Lee, I told you to stay away from me."

"I know, but I can't do that." In the face of her anger, which he more than deserved, he flinched. "Like I told you, I'm gonna make things right between us, whatever I have to do. And you can yell and cuss, all you want, but if I see something I can do for you, I'm gonna do it."

"Why?" Tears welled in her blue eyes, and

that was the last thing he wanted, as her emotions gnawed at his conscience. "It's been three years. Why now?"

"Because I can't live with myself. Because the memory of that night haunts me." Despite his humiliation, and her desire to be rid of him, which was nothing compared to what he'd done to her, he had to tell her the truth, and the hell with the consequences. "I should have taken you with me, to the party. I should've stood up to my friends and been proud to be seen with you. Instead, I was a coward, and I hate myself for what I did, because you didn't deserve that, and I was crazy about you."

For a while, she just stared him, and he wanted to shrivel up and die, on the spot.

"You were?" When Russ nodded, she inclined her head. "Why didn't you say anything? Why did you trash me, instead?"

"The easy answer is peer pressure, but that's a copout." Doubling over from the pain she projected, he gritted his teeth. "I'm sorry, Cindy. I'm so sorry. I wish I could go back and undo it, but I can't. I can only move forward as I should have, then."

"Hey, are you okay?" The agony faded, when she rested her hand to his forearm. "You don't look so good."

"I'm all right." In that instant, she reflected nothing but concern, and he ached to kiss her. To hold her. "Granny wanted me to invite you over for dinner, again. I think she wants to talk to you about the wedding."

"I don't know, Russell." Even as she questioned herself, her inner desire was to help him. After all he'd done to her, she still cared about him.

How could he have made such a terrible mistake?

"Please, Cindy." He wanted to reach out to her. To take her in his arms and console her, but she didn't want that. "I know you're mad at me, and you have every right to be, but don't take out your anger on Minnie. It's not her fault."

"I know, and I'd never do anything to hurt your grandmother." She carried her bike up the steps and propped the old ten-speed against the rail. "Let me change my shoes, wash my face, and put on a nice sweater."

"Sure." Like a nervous but hopeful boyfriend, Russ waited for her, as he might have had he made another choice when they were kids. To distract himself, he gathered his rake, yard gloves, and extra trash bags. Finally, he sat on the top stair. When he could no longer take the anticipation, he stood.

"You could have come inside."

When he peered over his shoulder, his knees buckled.

"Wow." His mouth watered. "You look beautiful."

"Thanks." After locking the door, she strolled to the sidewalk, and he followed her to Minnie's.

Although Cindy gave off some definite stress, he didn't sense the same disgust she projected at the hospital, and that encouraged him, as they joined his granny.

"Why does it always take you so long to fetch Cindy, when all I do is give her a holler, and she comes running?" Minnie carried a covered pot to the table, which had been set with her best china, a lace cloth, and two candlesticks. "Sit down, before my delicious mostaccioli, made from my mother's recipe, gets cold."

"Bet it's so good it'll slap you." Cindy stuck her tongue in her cheek, as she pulled out a chair. "And that garlic bread smells incredible."

Something in Minnie's demeanor struck Russ as odd, and he couldn't put a finger on it until she dished two portions. For some strange reason, she delayed serving herself.

The phone rang.

"Infernal clap trap. Russell Lee, pour the wine. I splurged and bought a bottle of Boone's Farm, in the Strawberry Hill flavor, just for the occasion." Minnie took off her apron, and he grew suspicious. "Start without me, and I'll be right back."

Yeah, right.

Then and there, he'd have bet the title to his Camaro that his granny was up to her usual mischief.

As he unscrewed the cap, he noted the crystal goblets, and he knew he'd been had.

"I didn't realize they still made that stuff," Cindy whispered. "My mom used to love it."

"I think I owe you another apology." He shook his head. "I could be wrong, but—"

"Well, I've always said that hospital couldn't function without me." Pressing a hand to her forehead, Minnie frowned. "I'm sorry to eat and run, but two nurses called in sick, and I've got to pull some OT."

"But, you didn't eat, Granny." Russ clenched his jaw. "Why don't you have a quick bite?"

"I can't, 'cause I've got to scoot, and I can buy a snack from the cafeteria." If he'd had any doubts as to her motives, that simple statement trounced them, because she always said she'd rather die than eat cafeteria food. Grabbing the keys to her hot pink VW Beetle, she waved. "Enjoy, and I'll see you in the morning."

The door slammed with a loud thud, all but screaming that he was alone with Cindy.

"You didn't know she was going to do that." It was a statement, not a question.

"No, I didn't." To his surprise, he sensed no anger or rejection from her. "But I'm really sorry. Minnie asked me if I'd done something to you, the other night, and I sort of brushed her off. I wonder if she was just trying to bring us together."

"It's okay." With her elbow atop the table, she rested her delicate chin in her palm. "Still, it might've been better if you'd just admitted you have no interest in me. That would've spared her a graveyard shift."

"What if I am interested in you?" He voiced the question before he noticed he spoke. "Would that be so bad?"

"We both know that's not true." Her pain resurfaced, and instinctively he covered her hand with his, but just as fast, she pulled away. "Don't."

"If you want to go home, I'll understand." When he stood, she grabbed his wrist and then withdrew. "I can pack some of the mostaccioli."

"No." Again, she took him by the wrist and gave him a gentle tug. "Sit down, and let's eat, because it'd be a shame to waste this lovely meal."

"Are you sure?" He sipped the wine, choked on the sickening sweetness, and pushed aside his glass. "I don't want to upset you."

"I think I can tolerate your company in exchange for Minnie's cooking." Ah, Cindy teased him like she did when they were kids.

Had Russ detected the tiniest bit of sadness or rejection, any desire to be rid of him, he'd have walked her home. Instead, she genuinely wanted to stay.

"Do you remember how we'd always work a double shift on Saturdays?" As he lifted his fork, his fingers shook. "We were together for twelve hours."

"We ruled the dining room." She averted her gaze and cast a hint of a smile. "Even when someone called in sick."

"We were a great team." It was then he wished he'd learned to manage his ability, because he had trouble separating his emotions from hers, and he couldn't read her. "We're still a great team."

"Yeah, but it was just a coincidence." After

selecting a chunk of garlic bread, she passed him the basket. "If I hadn't been scheduled at the same time as you, you'd have handled the tavern with someone else."

"Do you really think it was a coincidence that we worked the same shifts every Saturday?" He snickered. "I arranged your hours to coincide with mine, on purpose, because I wanted to be close to you, no matter the circumstance."

She paused, mid-chew. "You didn't."

"I did." He jutted his chin. "And I looked forward to our Saturdays, all week."

"Why didn't you say anything?" With a heavy sigh, she put down her fork and grasped the edge of the table. "I'm so confused, Russ, because none of this seems logical. All you had to do was talk to me. Was that asking so much?"

"Cindy, I was a young, horny jock." That was putting it mildly. "Conversation wasn't a priority."

"But, if you liked me, why did you say those awful things about me?" Her pain returned. "How could you do that to me, after I chose you as my first?"

"Because I was stupid, too." In that instant, Rafe's words echoed in Russell's ears, *I don't bang George, I make love to her. Maybe one day you'll grow up and learn the difference.* "And you deserved better than the backseat of my car. I should've done it right. I should've bought you a dozen roses, taken you to dinner at The Judges Chambers, and got a room."

"Except it wasn't planned." She furrowed her brow. "It was a split-second decision."

"Why did you let me have you that night?" In his mind, he recalled her shy expression, as she nodded, after he coaxed her into his Camaro. "Hell, I was shocked when you let me cop a feel."

"It was no secret you were leaving Haven Harbor," she said, in a small voice. "If I was going to do it with anyone, I wanted it to be you, and I figured it was my last chance."

"You gave me a precious gift." No matter how hard he tried, he could never equal her worth. "And then I pulled that jackass stunt." He could just kick himself. "But I'd give anything to make it up to you. You don't have to forgive me, and I wouldn't even ask it of you. I just want a chance to make it right."

"How?" she asked, with more than a little skepticism.

"I don't know, but I'd sure like to try." Russ stretched his arm and touched his finger to hers, and she didn't pull away. "Please, Cindy. We could start over, as friends."

Minnie's grandfather clock, which she'd had custom made, chimed the hour, to the tune of the chorus from Clarence Henry's "Ain't Got No Home," her favorite song. Granny came honestly by her eccentricities.

When the house fell quiet, he pretty much accepted defeat.

"Okay."

~

After shrugging into her jacket and raincoat, Cindy pulled on her gloves, stepped onto the porch, and locked the door, just as headlights illuminated the house, and she glanced over her shoulder. In the driveway, Russell Lee sat in his Camaro, and he rolled down the window.

"Need a ride, pretty lady?" How anyone could look that gorgeous that early was beyond her. "Come on, it's damp and freezing, but it's nice and warm in here."

"How will I get home?" Wondering whatever possessed her to accept his offer of truce, she peered at the sky, as lightning flashed overhead. "I don't want to be any trouble."

"You could never be any trouble." To her surprise, he got out of the car, skipped up the steps, grabbed her hand, led her to the passenger side, opened the door, pushed her to the seat, secured her safety belt, closed her in, and then ran around to the driver's side. "And I'll bring you home, because we're working the same hours."

"Is that on purpose?" Laughing, she recalled their conversation, over dinner. "Or is it just an accident?"

"What do you think?" He winked, and the implication was unmistakable. How she wanted to believe in him. Needed to have faith in him. "And I don't like you riding your bike, alone, at this hour. It's dangerous. If you need to go somewhere, just give me a holler on my cell."

"Seriously? This is Haven Harbor, not Boston." Of course, she'd never been beyond the city limits, so she really didn't know the difference, but she was touched by his concern. "And I don't have your number."

"Here." He tossed her his phone. "Call yourself, and put me in your contacts."

"Okay, but you're being ridiculous, because I've biked everywhere, since I was a kid." Even as she did what he asked, she doubted he'd stick with the crack-of-dawn wake-ups, and she'd be right back on her trusty ten-speed. "Besides, if I get really desperate, I'll drive my mom's old Charger."

"Wait, you have a Charger?" As they

stopped for a red light, he glanced at her. "Now that's a real muscle car. What year is it?"

"It's a sixty-seven, in electric blue, with black leather interior." And it was a monster gas-guzzler, which is why she rarely took it out of the garage. "It was my grandpa's pride and joy."

"I bet." After pulling into the tavern parking lot, he turned off the ignition, jumped out, and opened her door before she could gather her purse and umbrella. "So when are you going to take me for a ride?"

"I'm not." She noted the empty space near the back entrance. "Can't believe we beat Tony here."

"Speak of the devil." As Russ unlocked the bolt, Tony slipped into his usual space. "Sleeping on the job?"

"Aw, boss two shows up early a second day, and I'm supposed to be impressed." The cook goosed Russ. "Why don't you make yourself useful and ice some cupcakes, while Cindy and I do the real work?"

"Hey, Tony, how did you survive infancy?" Russ donned an apron. "And aren't your parents cousins?"

"All right, that's enough." For Cindy, it was just like the old days, before graduation.

Before her hero disappointed her. "Don't make me separate you."

"Yeah, you don't want to piss me off." Russ strutted to the sink, to wash some blueberries, and she admired his ass. No matter what he did to her, he was still a nice specimen, and some small part of her wanted him. "I might have to fire you, in my sister's absence."

"You talk to her last night?" The conversation grew serious, as Tony threw several strips of bacon into a skillet. "How's she doing?"

"She's George." As Russ set a bag of flour on the counter, he snorted. "From what I hear, Rafe really read her the riot act, because it looks like she's a couple month's pregnant. So she's gonna stay home, until Monday, and then she'll work part-time until Rafe says otherwise."

"That's what he thinks." Just then, Mary-George strolled into the kitchen. "I'm not so delicate, and he's making mountains out of molehills."

"George, what are you doing here?" Casting a nasty scowl, Tony wiped his hands on a towel. "You've got a bun in the oven, and you're supposed to be in bed."

"Does Rafe know you're here?" Arching a

brow, Russ rested fists on hips. "Is he okay with this?"

"I'm fine, and he's at the hospital, so what he doesn't know won't hurt him." Just then, her phone rang, and she pressed a finger to her lips to quiet the group. "Hi, honey. Oh, I'm just lying around, watching television." When Russ snickered, she gave him the stink-eye, and he stuck his tongue at her. "No, I'm not planning on doing much of anything. Why? Lunch? Sounds dreamy. Okay, I'll see you then. I love you, too." As she ended the call, she wiped her temple. "Whew, that was a close one."

"If he finds out you broke out of the house, he's gonna be pissed." Tony whistled. "Then you'll find out who rules the roost."

"Stop it." Glancing left and then right, she huffed a breath. "What can I do?"

"Go home." Tony filled a huge pot with water. "We've got this, and boss two is in training as Cindy's sous-chef."

"Well, they make a cute couple." Given Mary-George knew nothing of what happened between Russ and Cindy, her comment bore no ill intent, but it hurt all the same. As Russ and Tony went about various tasks, Mary-George walked to Cindy. "When's the appointment at the bank?"

"Tomorrow." Excited at the prospect, Cindy bounced on her heels. "Oh, Mary-George, I want this. I want to open a bakery, so bad."

"You're going to be great, and I'll support you however I can." Mary-George narrowed her stare. "What if you continue to supply all the desserts for the tavern, and we advertise your business?"

"What a wonderful idea." Cindy considered the benefits and the possibility of returning the favor. "I could create different pastries to compliment various beers, and how about I cross-promote the tavern?"

"That would be fantastic." George extended a hand. "It's a deal."

As Cindy accepted the gesture, she glanced up—and noticed Rafe standing in the doorway. "Uh-oh, someone's busted."

"What's wrong?" When Mary-George gazed over her shoulder, she flinched. "Hi, honey. What are you doing here?" Slowly, she rounded the counter and approached her fiancé. "I came in to make sure they didn't need me."

Rafe folded his arms but said nothing.

"Turns out they have everything under control, so I was just about to go home." George hugged him about the waist.

"No, she wasn't." Tony smirked. "Don't let her fool you, Rafe."

"Tattletale." Mary-George pouted. "I just wanted to help prepare for the lunch rush, and I feel fine."

"George, you're pregnant." Finally, he relented and embraced her, and Cindy envied the love so obvious in their interaction. She wanted a relationship like that, once. And she wanted it with Russell Lee, but that dream died a long time ago. "Whether or not you're willing to accept it, you're resting for two, now. If you won't take care of yourself for your own sake, then do it for our child."

In that instant, Cindy wondered how it felt to have someone dote on her. To have a man put her health and welfare before all else. She'd never known that sort of devotion.

"You make me sound selfish, when you put it that way." As Rafe cradled George's head, she sighed. "I'm sorry, and I'll go home."

"To be sure, I'm going to drive you, and I'll get your brother to fetch your truck, later." Cupping her chin, he kissed her forehead. "Where's your purse and coat? It's pouring out there, and I don't want to risk you catching a cold."

"In the office." On tiptoes, she pressed her lips to his. "Give me a second, and I'll be right back."

"Okay, baby." When George cleared the room, Rafe said to Russ, "If you'll drive the truck to the house, I'll bring you back to the tavern."

"Actually, that's not necessary." Russ elbowed Cindy. "Pretty Miss Parker can follow me, in the Camaro."

Cindy thought she might faint at the prospect of sitting behind the wheel of his car.

"You're a lifesaver." Rafe turned to walk out, but he paused. "Do me a favor and keep the keys."

"Will do." Russ saluted. "Hey, how'd you know she was here?"

"Location services on her cell." Frowning, Rafe shook his head. "I knew she'd pull a stunt like this."

"If you come by around noon, I'll have some food packed up for you." Tony wielded a wooden spoon like a weapon. "And don't worry, I'll make it nice and healthy—with no flavor."

"Thanks, Tony." Rafe chuckled. "I appreciate it."

Soon, quiet fell on the kitchen, and the threesome got down to business, churning out a huge assortment of comfort food, including Tony's killer three-alarm chili, which paired great with Cindy's homemade cornbread and the Goblin Grolsch beer.

The next thing she knew, the wait staff appeared, which meant it was time to open the doors, and they had a line down the sidewalk. As the hostess seated customers, Cindy grabbed her ticket book. Working in unison with Russ, they greeted and served half the dining room, and she enjoyed every minute of it—until she welcomed her next table.

"Good afternoon." Bracing for the usual lewd comments, she focused on her notes, as Brian and Shane, two of Russ's former teammates, leered. "Today's special is chicken and dumplings, and the featured dessert is apple pie. Are you ready to order?"

"I'd like a soft, juicy taco." Shane snickered. "One of the pink variety."

"We don't serve tacos, sir." She bit her tongue against a cutting remark. "May I suggest the fish and chips?"

"Aw, come on, Cindy." Brian smiled his slimy smile. "When are you going to stop playing hard to get and go out with me? I mean, it's not as if you've got better offers."

"Hey, knock it off." To her shock, Russ grabbed her by the arms and set her aside. "If you can't treat her with the respect she deserves, then you don't talk to her."

"Russell, my man, I heard you were back in town." Brian extended a hand, but Russ just stood there. "You back to slumming? I don't blame you, 'cause I'd pay big money for a taste of that piece of ass."

"Get out." As Cindy hugged the wall, Russ lunged and grabbed Brian by the shirt collar. "If I catch you near her again, I'll put you in the hospital, if you're lucky."

"Whoa." Shane splayed his palms. "We were just having fun. We didn't mean anything by it."

"I don't care." Russ shoved Brian toward the exit. "You're banned from the tavern."

Lingering in the shadows, Cindy couldn't believe how Russ came to her rescue and defended her, when his behavior inspired the crude comments. Cracking open the door, she eavesdropped on the confrontation.

"You don't know her." Despite the torrential downpour, Russ loomed on the sidewalk and speared his fingers through his hair. "And I lied. I never touched her, because she's too good for me, and she's damn sure too good for you, now get out of here."

When he turned, she ran into the bar, which didn't open until noon. As he crossed in front of the hostess stand, he spotted her.

"You okay?" Dripping wet, he wiped his face.

"Yes." From behind the bar, she retrieved a towel and handed it to him. "Why did you do that?"

Gently, he trailed a finger along the curve of her cheek. "I told you, I'm gonna make this right."

CHAPTER THREE

Two weeks had passed since Russ returned home, and he'd fallen into a nice, comfortable routine, despite the unexpected revelation that he was going to be an uncle, which hastened George's wedding. In fact, everything in his life revolved around the ceremony, which had been moved to the community center, the upcoming weekend, much to Minnie's delight and Rafe's mother's loudly expressed displeasure.

Given the somewhat managed chaos, George surrendered control of the tavern to Russ, and with Cindy's help, the restaurant thrived. While he appreciated her dedication, and he relied on her, she really stepped up her game, and more than anything he just enjoyed being near her. To his surprise, he caught himself imagining all sorts of possibilities for the future, and every one of them involved Cindy Parker.

"Hey, Russ, are you listening to me?" Standing in the doorway to her en suite, George clapped her hands. Gowned in white, she rotated. "Tell me the truth, what do you think of this one?"

"Wow." It was hard to believe his big sis was getting married in a dress, because she'd spent the better part of her life in tattered jeans and Converse tennis shoes. "You gonna wear makeup, too?"

"Yeah." Checking her appearance in a mirror, she bit her lip and smoothed her palms over her hips. "Does this make me look fat?"

"Is that a trick question?" He shrugged. "I mean, you're eventually going to pork out because of the kid, right?"

"Oh, that's so lovely." She sighed. "I don't know why I ask you anything."

"Hey, I wanted to thank you for not reaming me over Cindy." After opening the tavern, he responded to a frantic call from his sister, only to discover hers was a fashion emergency. As she tried on each of the six gowns she borrowed from the Happily Ever After Bridal Shoppe, he confessed what happened three years ago, on graduation night. "I figured you'd blow a gasket."

"I would've, if you didn't look like you've been beating yourself up over what you did." Pinning a veil at the crown her hair, George shook her head. "But I wish I'd known what happened, because I've been trying to set you up with her, forever. She's a nice girl, and I still can't believe what you did."

"Neither can I, but I'm gonna make it right." Just then, he glanced at his watch. "Shit. Her meeting at the bank is in forty-five minutes. I need to get back to the tavern, because I want to wish her luck."

"Russ, just a second." Covered in silk and lace, George walked to him and rested her hands to his shoulders. "I know you're sorry for what you did, but I don't think that's all you're feeling. I suspect you care about her more than you're letting on, and you need to tell her, because it could make all the difference in the world."

"Look, I blew my chance, and I know it. She'll never believe in me, again, and I don't deserve her." Downstairs, he pulled on his raincoat. "Damn, it's coming down in sheets, and she planned to walk to the bank. I better get back, in case she needs a ride."

"Okay." George kissed his cheek. "But don't give up on her. I thought Rafe would never forgive me for hiding the truth about my gift, and he did. On Saturday, you're going to walk me down the aisle, and he's going to become my husband. And next May, we're going to welcome our first child. Nothing's lost until it's really gone, Russ. You and Cindy are still here."

"Thanks, sis." He pressed his lips to her forehead. "I love you."

With his head bowed, he ran to his car, jumped inside, shoved the key into the ignition, cranked the engine, and flipped on the windshield wipers. After a quick ride into town, he pulled into the tavern parking lot. As he rushed through the back door, something dawned on him. A way to show Cindy that she meant more to him than she realized.

"Hey, boss two, how's George?" At the counter, Tony peeled a potato, in preparation for the dinner menu. "She pick out a wedding dress, yet?"

"Yeah, I think she's made her decision." Russ glanced left and then right. "Where's Cindy?"

"In the break room, Romeo." The cook waggled his brows. "When are you gonna man up and ask her on a date?"

"Tony, if you had another brain it would be

lonely." Then again, he couldn't afford to alienate a possible co-conspirator. "She's got better things to do than waste time with me, but I'd like to do something for her, if you'll do something for me—well, for Cindy."

"Sure, kid." In some ways, Tony was that weird uncle everybody loved but didn't really want to be around, because he was rude, crude, loud, and smelled funny, but he'd give the shirt off his back if he thought someone needed it. "What you got in mind?"

"You know she's got that meeting with the loan officer, today." When Tony nodded, Russ formed a plan. "She's pulling a double with me, and she'll need to eat before the dinner rush, but she won't have a lot of time. I was wondering if you might help me set up a meal for her."

For a second, he held his breath in anticipation of some wise-ass remark, but Tony said nothing. Then he scratched his chin.

"You know, ladies like flowers, especially roses." Narrowing his stare, the cook wrinkled his nose. "We could put a table for two in the back corner of the bar, near the jukebox."

"That's a great idea." Russ snapped his fingers. "And I'll run to—"

"Okay, I'm ready to go." Wearing khaki slacks, a white dress shirt, and a navy blue blazer, with her blonde hair in a bun, Cindy met his stare, and he sensed just how important the bakery was to her, because she wanted it bad. "I just hope I don't drown on the way."

"Take my car." He handed her the keys. "And you're gonna be a hit."

"Are you sure?" She bit her bottom lip, and he ached to run his tongue along the length of her mouth. "The streets are slick. What if I have a wreck?"

"I'm insured, so just be sure nothing happens to you." He winked. "Everything else can be replaced."

"All right." Why didn't she want him to know she was thrilled to drive the Camaro? "I'll be back in plenty of time for the dinner rush."

"Aw, why don't you two just get it over with and kiss?" Tony smooched the air. "Good luck, Cindy."

"Just relax, and be yourself. The bakery is a fantastic idea. It's a winner, and they'll know that." After walking her to the door, and waving as she drove away, Russ turned to Tony. "Now, let's get to work."

In the dark corner of the bar, Tony

arranged a table and two chairs, while Russell fetched a white tablecloth and matching napkins. From the main dining room, he collected a couple of candles and silverware.

"Now, why don't you run to the florist, and I'll put together a menu." Wielding a rolling pin, the cook clucked his tongue. "And don't be a cheap bastard. Spring for the roses, because she's worth it." Then Tony tossed his keys to Russ. "Take Bessie, but be gentle with her, because she's a classic lady."

"Don't worry." In seconds, Russ darted to the dented green Vega, unlocked the door, and slid behind the wheel. When he turned the ignition, the engine choked, screamed, and died. He went through three attempts before the car idled.

The trip to The Enchanted Florist proved tricky, as the Vega constantly stalled, but he finally made it. Inside, he walked past several refrigerated cases, which contained all kinds of flowers, including some he'd never seen. At the last display, he located roses in every conceivable color, and what had seemed a simple task became daunting.

"May I help you?" a saleslady asked.

"Yeah, I'd like to buy a dozen roses." That should've been easy, but the selection overwhelmed him.

"In what shade?" Again, she stumped him.

"Well, that's a good question." One for which he had no answer. "Do they have a particular meaning?"

"Oh, yes, but we would be here all night, were I to try and explain the significance of our entire inventory." Pointing, she smiled. "Yellow expresses friendship. Coral conveys desire. Pink reflects admiration. White is typically reserved for brides. And, of course, the classic red represents love." When he didn't immediately respond, she clasped her hands in front of her. "Perhaps, you should consider the recipient. What does she mean to you?"

"I'll take a dozen red roses." Pulling his wallet from his back pocket, he approached the counter. "And I'd like them arranged in a nice vase."

"How about I add some lovely purple snapdragons to compliment the rich crimson tone?" The saleslady tapped her chin. "And I have an elegant crystal vase, which I can highlight with a beautiful bow."

"Thank you." He passed her his credit card. "That sounds great."

Twenty minutes later, bouquet in hand, Russ returned to the Vega, belted the arrangement in the passenger seat, and sped back to the tavern.

"Wow." In the kitchen, Tony chopped some carrots, but he paused to admire the roses. "You really outdid yourself, kid. Cindy's gonna love those. I've got everything prepared, so why don't you put those on the table, and I'll send her to the bar as soon as she comes through that door. Oh, and don't forget to breathe, or you'll drop dead."

"Okay." Exhaling, Russ rolled his shoulders, strolled down the hall, pushed through the double doors, and walked into the bar.

At the little table for two, he put the vase in the center. Then he moved it to the right. Then he pushed it to the left. Then he scooted it closer to the wall. At last, he returned it to the center.

Nervous, he paced, sat, stood, and twiddled his thumbs. Checking his watch, he wondered what was taking so long.

A thought occurred to him.

If Cindy secured the financing for a bakery, she would be quitting the tavern. No more carpooling. No more working together in the kitchen. No more tag-teaming the dining room.

No more Cindy.

He wasn't sure how he felt about that, aside

from the gut-wrenching pain. Just when it seemed he'd made some headway in their relationship, she was leaving him.

"Tony said you needed to see me." Cindy lingered in the entry from the foyer. When she spotted the flowers, she looked at him. "What's all this?"

"Surprise." Splaying his arms, he smiled. "I arranged a quiet dinner for us. How'd it go?"

In that instant, she burst into tears.

"Hey, what happened?" To his shock, she ran straight at him, hugged him about his waist, and buried her face in his chest. While he hated the fact that she was so upset, he was damn happy to have her in his arms. "What'd they say?"

"Oh, Russ, it was awful." She sniffed. "The loan officer said that because I have no credit history, I need sufficient collateral to secure the note, and the house isn't enough, or I need to find someone to finance my bakery. What am I going to do?"

"Shh." For some reason he couldn't begin to fathom, he bent his head and kissed her. Cindy could have slapped him. She could have pulled free. Instead, she opened to him.

For several intense minutes, he sucked on her sweet tongue, nipped her bottom lip, and extended comfort in that kiss, and she let him.

And never had Russ felt more like a man.

There was power in the exchange, and he realized he wanted to be her hero. He wanted to give her the world, but he'd bet she'd be happy with a bakery.

"Listen, you need to eat something, before we open for the dinner service." As would a gentleman, he held her chair, and she sat. "Don't worry about the bank, because we'll figure out something."

"The roses are beautiful." She wiped a tear from her cheek. "Thank you."

"You're welcome." As she toyed with a perfect bud, he fished his cell phone from his jeans and texted his sister.

Russell Lee: The bank turned down Cindy's loan, and I need to talk to you.

~

In the wake of her disappointment, Cindy focused her efforts on George's wedding. As the official cake designer, she devoted hours to a custom creation that could increase her business. Of course, she'd have to make do with the tight space in the tavern's gift shop, for the foreseeable future, and that was all right with her. Eventually, she'd open her bakery.

As she waited on the oven timer, and the

last layer of the five tiers to bake, she pulled her wish book, the ruffled edges comprised of countless sticky notes, each representing part of her dream, from her tote. Flipping through the pages, she reflected on her goal and everything she'd done to make it happen, yet she failed, and she wanted to cry at the unfairness of the situation. Still, she'd vowed she'd find a way to make it happen. Maybe, after she earned her degree.

"What's that?" Peering over her shoulder, Russ rested his hands to her hips and kissed the crest of her ear, something he did with more frequency since the evening they shared dinner in the bar, and he still startled her. Yet, something grew between them. Something mystical and powerful, and hope blossomed in that tiny space in her heart she reserved just for him. "Did you schedule a meeting at one of the other banks in town? Who knows, you might get a different answer."

"I already tried." At his expression of surprise, she shrugged. "I was embarrassed, so I didn't say anything. I figured I'd tell you if I was approved, and we could really celebrate. But Bank of America declined my application for financing, for the same reasons, and Newburyport wouldn't even give me an appointment, after I filled out the initial interest card."

"Aw, babe, I'm sorry." That was another recent development. He called her by terms of endearment, and she liked it more than she was willing to admit. It was strange how something so simple could mean so much. "Hey, I know you'll be busy during the ceremony, tomorrow, but I wondered if you'd save me a dance."

"Sure." While she'd never forget what he did to her, three years ago, things had changed between them. They'd grown up, and he wasn't the same guy who took her virginity in the backseat of his Camaro. Instead, he projected a sweetness, a softness—a vulnerability she couldn't resist, and she'd save all her dances for him, if he asked her. Then again, she could never say no to him, no matter how bad he hurt her. "And this is the restaurant supply catalogue."

"What's with all the sticky notes?" He opened to one of the makeshift bookmarks. "Black and white striped window awning."

"Okay, don't laugh." Despite what occurred between them, she shared some of her most cherished dreams with him, and he worked hard to improve the tavern. "You know that empty storefront at the corner of

Birch and Oak?"

"Yep." He nodded. "Across from the bookstore, right?"

"That's it." If he made fun of her, she'd kill him. "The window-front is divided by the entrance, and I'd like the awning to span the whole length, to make the bakery stand out, almost like a French patisserie, with coordinating décor." She turned to another page. "And I'd buy a custom-carved wood sign to display the name, Sweet & Spooky Bakery."

"Sweet & Spooky?" He quirked his brows and stared at her, and she held her breath in anticipation of some taunting remark. Slowly, he smiled. "It's catchy."

"Do you think so?" Biting her bottom lip, she perched on tiptoes, because she needed his approval. She didn't know why she felt that way, but she just did. "You're not just saying it because you know it's what I want to hear?"

"If it didn't work, I'd tell you." As he scanned her selections, he narrowed his stare. "The tables are a nice touch, but I'd wait on those, because we have a stash in the warehouse. Instead, you should focus on purchasing those items that will help build your brand, like the frilly, custom printed tablecloths and your packaging. Then you could spend more money on ingredients, because your product is everything. While the exterior will get them in the store; your baked goods will keep them coming back."

"What a great idea." As she started to make a note, she paused, because reality punched her in the nose. "At least, it would be, if I had a bakery."

"Hey, don't give up." He kissed her forehead and pulled her close, to nudge her nose.

That was all the invitation she needed, and she lifted her chin ever so slightly to offer her lips.

As always, Russ smelled of Old Spice, which she remembered from high school, and tasted of some sort of strong, minty mouthwash, as he mingled his tongue with hers, and she craved his attention. Soft and tender, he brushed his flesh to hers, and it was a treat that he initiated more and more, much to her delight.

Yet, even though he hugged Cindy tight, and spent most of his time with her, he hadn't asked her to be his date for the wedding or the annual Samhain Ball, and she'd already bought killer dresses for both events. To her chagrin, nagging doubt crept into her brain, and she retreated.

"Listen, you know I have to take George to the wedding, because she banished Rafe to the Old Haven Mill Hotel, with his parents, so he won't see her gown until she arrives at the community center." Was it her imagination, or did he just read her mind? Surely, she didn't voice her thoughts. "And I know you'll be busy transporting the cake, because Tony said he's acting as your assistant, using his wife's minivan. If you were free, I'd ask you to be my date."

"Well, we don't have to ride together to be dates, do we?" Pressing her palms to his muscled chest, she inclined her head and wished with everything inside her for what she most desired, in that moment. "We can partner at the ceremony."

"Yes, we can." When he bared his boyish smile, her heart melted. "So, you're going with me?"

"I am, indeed." It dawned on Cindy then that the wedding would be their first real date, and she resolved to pay extra attention to her hairstyle and makeup, because she wanted to look pretty for him. The oven timer pinged. "That's my last tier, and by the time it cools, I'll have the other four layers iced and decorated. And when I set up the whole thing at the community center, I'll trim each layer in piped pearls, to give it a finished look, and then I'll add a cascade of sugar flowers to complete the design. It's a technique I learned from my mom, and she's the reason I bake. It was something we shared on her days off."

"Hey, I was wondering why you never mention your father." Oblivious to her gut-wrenching agony, Russ stuck his finger in the buttercream frosting and sampled it. "Mmm, this is heaven." Then he sobered. "What is it? What did I say?"

"I never knew my father." And it was a secret she'd long hidden, because kids could be cruel. "He left before I was born."

"What do you mean he left?" Leaning against the counter, Russ tucked a stray lock of hair beneath her net. "Where'd he go?"

"I don't know." She shrugged, as the memory sent a chill down her spine. "Guess he didn't want to be a father, because when my mom told him she was pregnant, he bailed."

"And he had no family, here?" He blinked. "Is there no one?"

"No." Shifting her weight, she grabbed a spatula and slathered the largest cake with buttercream, because she needed a distraction.

A TASTE OF MAGICK

"My mom moved here, from Boston, before I was born, and she never talked about her past. I think it was uncomfortable for her."

"I'm so sorry, Cindy." With the backs of his knuckles, he caressed her cheek. "I shouldn't have asked, because it's none of my business."

"It's okay." To her surprise, he took the spatula from her grasp, set it aside, and again drew her into his arms. "Really, it's fine."

"I don't think so." Cradling her head, he rocked from side to side. "And then I shit on you, when that was the last thing you needed from a guy. If it makes you feel any better, no matter what happens between us, I'll always be here for you."

"Don't feel sorry for me, because I'm not a charity case, Russ." But she'd take one of his hugs any day of the week and twice on Sunday, because she loved listening to his heartbeat. "I'm going to earn my degree in accounting and figure out how to finance my bakery. It may not happen today, it may not happen next year, but it will happen."

Just then, her cell phone rang, and she tugged it from her pocket.

"Go ahead." He released her.

As she accepted the call, he poked her in the ribs, and she yelped. "Hello."

"May I speak with Miss Cindy Parker, please?" an unknown man inquired.

"This is Cindy." She swatted Russ's hand, as he jabbed at her belly.

"Miss Parker, this is Dean Connelly, of the Common Ground Savings and Loan. I told you I'd search for financing options, to fund your business note, and I've found an investor willing to back your venture."

"What?" In that instant, she grabbed Russ by the wrist and met his stare. "Can you say that again?"

"Of course." Mr. Connelly chuckled. "I imagine I caught you off guard, but I promised I'd try to secure a small business loan, and I've done it."

"Oh, Mr. Connelly, I don't know what to say except thank you." She bounced with joy, as Russ mouthed, *What.* "Thank you, so much. Now, what's the next step? What do I need to do?"

"Why don't you stop by my office on Monday, around nine, if it's convenient, and I'll have the paperwork ready for you to sign."

"I'll put you on my calendar." When Russ stuck his tongue at her, she mirrored his move. "And thank you, again, Mr. Connelly. This means the world to me."

"You're welcome, Miss Parker. I'll see you

A TASTE OF MAGICK

on Monday."

As soon as she hung up, she jumped Russell Lee.

"I got it." Showering his face in kisses, she laughed. "I got the loan."

CHAPTER FOUR

"How'd it go with Mr. Connelly?" As George adjusted her veil, she glanced at Russ. "Did Cindy ask any questions? Does she suspect anything?"

Since his sister was his co-conspirator, he couldn't ignore her, although he really didn't want to talk about the manipulations he contrived, in order to give Cindy her dream. But he couldn't sit by and do nothing, when he had the ability and the funds to give her what she wanted.

"He said she was so excited that she couldn't sit still, as he reviewed the terms of the loan, and she just signed the documents, without much debate." Reflecting on the scheme he managed to pull off, he couldn't stop smiling, yet he feared the consequences when Cindy discovered the identity of the owners behind the quickly created 2M Capital Group, which didn't exist a week ago. "In fact, when he explained that she'd landed a small business grant, intended to revitalize the area, which covered a year's rent, she didn't bat an eyelash. And when she recounted the story to me, she didn't doubt any part of it. Then she cried, because she was so happy."

Later, she dragged him—well, maybe he dragged her, into the stockroom, where she kissed him for the better part of a half an hour, behind a huge stack of boxes, but that was his secret. And she let him cop a feel of her breasts, as well as her tight ass, and he almost blew his wad in his jeans, as she speared her fingers in his hair, because everything inside her declared she wanted him. While he wanted much more from Cindy, he didn't want to rush her. Instead, he took his time and pursued her, as he should have when they were in high school.

"Oh, Russ, I'm so glad we could do that for her, because she deserves it, and she's going to be a massive success, so it's a great investment for us." Gowned in her wedding dress, his sister neared and took his hands in hers. "I hate to bring this up on my special day, but you know you're going to have to tell her the truth, at some point. Don't keep secrets from her, because it'll make it worse when she finds out what you did for her, and she'll eventually find out."

That was the one part of his plan hadn't addressed, because he honestly didn't know how to resolve the situation. And he feared the repercussions, because he couldn't lose Cindy.

"Why didn't you tell me we owned all that property downtown?" That had been one hell of a shock, because he thought the tavern was their lone inheritance. "I had no idea we were that rich."

"Well, for one thing, you never asked about the finances, and I left Mr. Harris in charge, because he was Mom and Dad's choice, so I trust him." With a sad expression, she averted her gaze. "Plus, you were young, and we were grieving, so there was no real need to involve you in the whole probate process. However, you're more than welcome to go through our holdings with Mr. Harris, any time, because it's your money, too. If you want to separate your half, that's fine. Believe me, there's plenty to divvy up, if that's your decision, and I'll support you."

"No, that's not necessary." With a sigh, he recalled the hug Cindy gave him, as she pressed her body to his, when she returned to the tavern. Soft and feminine in his arms, she blushed, as he trailed his tongue along the curve of her lips. "I'm just not sure how I'm going to share all this with her, because things are going great for us, and I don't want to screw it up." Shuffling his feet, he rubbed the back of his neck. "Ah, hell, I think I'm in love with her."

"You think?" She snorted and rolled her eyes. "Brother, I can read it in everything you do. You're head over heels for Cindy Parker, and I couldn't be more thrilled."

"Yeah, I am, but the tavern and the bakery—it all means nothing if I don't have her." Anxious, because he had so much to lose, he paced near the window. "She wants me, George. She wants me bad, and I sense it whenever she's around. I just don't want to disappoint her, because I've already hurt her."

"What do you mean you sense it?" In that instant, he halted and met his sister's stare, and she sobered. "Russell Lee Aaron McBride, you have the gift."

Trying but failing to mask his emotions, he turned his back to his sister. "No, I just—"

"Don't even try to deny it, because you're all but screaming the truth, and you know you can't hide from me." Grabbing him by the shoulders, she rotated him to face her. "Why didn't you say anything? Why didn't you tell me? How long have you struggled with your ability?"

"Since we were kids." And he hated admitting it, because he didn't want to be a witch. "But I don't struggle." When she arched a brow, he blew out breath. "Okay, I did, at first, but I've learned to block it, and it really doesn't bother me, now."

"Liar." She frowned. "You're hurting right now, and no one knows better than me what you're feeling." Her phone pinged, and she snatched it from the dresser. "Oh, crap. It's Rafe. I never should've given him access to my account, because he knows we haven't left the house, and he's panicking." As she typed a response, she snickered. "His parents are driving him nuts, and he can't wait to get out of town."

"Then we'd better hit the road." Grateful for the distraction, he scooped her lace train and followed in her wake, as she descended the stairs. "Where'd you two decide to honeymoon?"

"Niagara Falls, for four days, although he warned me I'd see little if any of the sights." After she slid into the passenger seat of the Camaro, he tucked her skirt around her.

A TASTE OF MAGICK

"We're leaving in the morning, because Rafe wants to consummate our vows here, at home. I think he's nervous, and I look forward to providing plenty of reassurance and validation."

"Okay, that's way more information than I want to know about my sister." Emanating raw desire, she laughed, and he wanted to hurl his guts. "I mean, I know you guys kick it, but I don't want to *know* about it."

"When did you become such a prude?" As he sped down River Road, she held onto her veil. "And how do you think I got knocked up?"

"I know how it happened, but I don't want to think about it, because it gives me the creeps." In his mind, an image flashed of Rafe going at her, and Russ shuddered. "I'd rather believe it's as Minnie used to say. You swallowed an egg, and it hatched in your belly."

"That's awful." Again, her phone pinged, and she checked her texts. "Poor Rafe. I'm coming, baby." Typing furiously, she bit her lip. "Just hold on, because we're almost there."

Minutes later, they pulled into the parking lot at the community center. Tony waved them into a spot near the front door.

"Hurry." The cook wiped his brow. "Man, am I glad to see you, because the doc is a nervous wreck, and he's been out here, twice, looking for you. If you make him wait much longer, I'm afraid he'll throw up, pass out, or both."

"I'm here, aren't I?" As they strolled into the foyer, George smoothed her skirt. "Are we ready?"

"Let me signal the musicians." Tony peered into the main hall and waved. "All right, George. You better get in there, before Rafe changes his mind, and you were lucky to land him."

The initial notes of Wagner's "Bridal Chorus" announced George's arrival, and the guests stood, as Tony pushed open the double doors.

"Very funny." Misty-eyed, she sniffed. "Now shut up, give me a kiss, and wish me well."

"Aw, boss lady, you know I love you like my own kin." Tony lifted the veil and gave her a quick peck on the cheek. "You look beautiful, and your parents would be so proud."

"Thank you, Tony." With her fingers, she daubed her face. "Okay, I guess this is it."

"Well, here goes nothing." Russ extended

A TASTE OF MAGICK

his arm, and George set her palm in the crook of his elbow. "Good luck, sis."

Together, they walked down the makeshift aisle, to the equally improvised arch made of PVC pipe covered in white macramé, with fall blooms tied together with eucalyptus at each corner, in the event hall where she organized the weekly potluck dinner to feed Haven Harbor's most vulnerable citizens. It was for that reason the place was packed to overflowing.

Looming at the other end was Rafe, and when he spied George, he grinned from ear to ear and wiped a stray tear. To Rafe's right stood Lucille Birkland, high priestess of the main Haven Harbor coven, and Pastor Devin Carruthers.

To the casual observer, the arrangement might have appeared strange, but not to a local. After Lucille performed the handfasting ritual, Pastor Carruthers would lead the traditional ceremony. No, that wasn't odd, because the witch community lived in peace alongside the civilian population.

That was the tongue-in-cheek joke, in Haven Harbor. Given the dark history surrounding witches and magick in America, the people of that small town embraced their unique heritage and diversity, poking fun at themselves, to divert attention from the truth.

But it was a joke that had been lost on Russ, because he wanted no part of it or his gift. He was a reluctant witch, at best. At Lucille's urging, he lifted George's veil, kissed her on the cheek, and said, "Knock 'em dead, sis. I love you."

In the front row, Cindy sat beside an empty chair, which she saved for him. As he took his place and settled himself, she reached for his hand and twined her fingers in his.

Immediately, a sense of calm washed over him as a gentle spring rain, and he relied on her to keep him grounded, as his sister moved on to the next chapter of her life. For some reason he couldn't understand, he felt very much alone in that moment.

"Friends and family of Mary-George and Rafe, on their behalf, we welcome you to their wedding in the Haven Harbor Community Center, in the heart of our fair city." Pastor Carruthers cleared his throat. "Let us remove ourselves from the routine of our everyday existence to witness a cherished moment in their lives, as the two become one."

"You did a great job," Cindy whispered.

Then he realized he wasn't alone. He had someone special of his own. In fact, he'd always had her—he just didn't know it.

A TASTE OF MAGICK

"Thanks." As he met and held her stare, a mystical web of emotion blanketed him in soothing warmth.

Opening himself to the experience, Russell shivered beneath the power of her desire—and something more. Something precious. While she wanted him, she harbored an emotional attachment, and he winked as he recognized the depth of her devotion. Then and there, he vowed that little Miss Parker would one day be Mrs. Russell Lee McBride.

~

Halloween, or Samhain, as the witch community called it, was Cindy's favorite holiday, because it held so many happy memories for her. While most people presumed Haven Harbor's embrace of all things witchy was more for the tourists than any real involvement in such mystical things, she knew otherwise.

Long ago, her mother explained that just because Cindy didn't understand something didn't mean it didn't exist. That magick—the real sort as designated by the –k, often manifested itself in the very things that usually inspired fear and doubt.

Yet it was our ability to have faith in that which we could not see that defined our humanity, when so many resorted to the rejection and destruction of that which they could not—would not comprehend. In walking the talk, Mama treated everyone with the same deference and kindness, and she taught her daughter to show the same respect for others.

Maybe that was why Russell's betrayal hurt so much.

It wasn't until the moment she crouched in the woods behind the tavern and witnessed his ruthless destruction of her character, just to appease his mean-spirited friends, that she realized not everyone shared her mother's sense of charity and acceptance. Of course, high school had been a rude study in the haves and the have nots, but she never let it bother her.

Why would she?

Still, as she walked into the Squeaky Cleaners to pick up her gown for the Samhain Ball, the singular event she looked forward to, every year, she coveted hope, and she smiled when her phone pinged.

Russell Lee: Hey, beautiful. Leaving the tavern. Pick you up at the bakery?

Cindy: I'm at the dry cleaners.

Russell Lee: Be right there.

Since signing on the dotted line on Monday, she'd launched a full-scale redo of her business. Although she'd offered to give two-week's notice to the tavern, Russ insisted she devote herself, full-time, to her venture. So, after a full day working on the interior of her modest shop, she'd finally finished painting the main dining area.

"It'll be eleven-fifty, Cindy." June Pascow, the owner, hung the teal blue gown on a stand. "Sure is a pretty dress. You wearing it to the ball, tonight?"

"That's the plan." Cindy handed June the exact amount and collected her plastic-wrapped garment. "Well, I'll see you there."

Now, if only Russ would ask her to the ball.

Outside, she spotted the Camaro parked on Mill Street, and she waved, as Russ jumped out to meet her. In fun, she ran straight into his outstretched arms, and he kissed her with a loud smack.

"Ready, beautiful?" As would a gentleman, he took the dress from her grasp, hung it on the hook in the back, and then held her door. "I missed you today. In fact, I miss you every day, at the tavern, and your customers are driving Tony crazy, asking for your baked goods."

"I miss you, too, and, if you want, I can go into the tavern, early in the morning, like I used to, and make a selection of items, which I'll continue to sell in the gift shop, until I open the bakery." In silence, she composed a schedule and ticked off various tasks, as he pulled away from the curb. "Then I can walk to the bakery and meet the workers, because I've got the new refrigerator going in on Monday, the display cases on Tuesday, and the office furniture should arrive on Wednesday. Oh, and I wanted to take you up on your offer to loan me some tables and chairs, because you were right, and my budget just doesn't allow for new ones, so I'll have to make do with what I can get."

"Whatever you need, beautiful." Reaching across the console, he grabbed her hand and brought it to his lips. "But I'll drive you, because you'll be doing me a huge favor, and that's quite a jaunt. How'd the meeting go with the restaurant supply guy?" In play, he nipped at her knuckles. "Did you get everything ordered?"

"No, but it went okay, I guess." Disappointed, she shrugged. "Half the things I wanted aren't in stock, and several items were on backorder, including the awning, so I doubt I'll have it in time for my grand opening, the week of Thanksgiving."

"Don't worry, because you'll be a hit

without it." As he turned onto Raven Road, he glanced at her and winked. "I dare anyone to resist your sweets, baby."

To her surprise, he pulled into Minnie's driveway, when he always took Cindy to her door. "I believe you forgot something."

"Actually, I didn't." After switching off the engine, he shifted and draped an arm about her shoulders. "Minnie's at work, and she'll be gone until the morning, so we've got the house to ourselves. I was thinking we could order a pizza, put a scary movie on the television, and hand out candy to the kids, because they'll be making the rounds tonight, instead of Tuesday."

"But—what about the Samhain Ball? The whole town will be there, except us." Crestfallen by the unwelcomed development, she pouted. "I bought a new dress just for the occasion, and I've always gone, ever since I was a kid."

"We can go next year, I promise." Why did she suspect that would never happen? "Besides, we'd just be bored, because there's nothing to do."

"Yes, there is." She huffed in frustration, because the conversation sounded vaguely familiar. "I look forward to the ball, all year, just like everyone else, and this one was supposed to be special, because I would share it with you, as your date."

"Well, I'm not going, and I don't want you to go, either." Nagging doubt seeped into her brain, festering and spoiling their recent interactions and what she thought was a budding relationship, as he extended a quick kiss. "I'll make it up to you, I promise. But I'd rather spend time alone with you, and that won't work with the ball. If we stay here, we can curl up on the couch, beneath a blanket, and I'll build a fire in the hearth. Doesn't that sound better than some stupid dance?"

While Russ proposed an intimate evening, all she heard was the faint echo of recriminations uttered three years ago, but she recalled the painful exchange in frightening detail, and it cut through her as though it happened yesterday.

Look, it's mainly my crew, and you'd be bored, so why don't you go home?

I just wanna hang with my buds, okay? And you're not my girlfriend or anything.

We screwed, big deal, because everybody does it.

I mean, I might have been your first, but I'm betting I won't be your last, so be cool, and I'll call you tomorrow.

Of course, he never called, and she waited by the phone until the very last second.

A TASTE OF MAGICK

Afterward, she cried all the way to the tavern, as she rode her bike. When she got to work, Mary-George asked if Cindy was okay, and she lied, claiming she had a nasty summer cold. Instead, she nursed a near fatal broken heart.

Why she'd thought he'd changed she couldn't begin to explain to herself, but it appeared she hadn't learned her lesson, because she'd once again fallen prey to his charm, and she found herself right where she started. Still, what he proposed offered her a chance for revenge, and it was a new and enticing sensation—one she couldn't resist.

"Sure, Russ." Cindy smiled, as she savored the taste of retribution. "Whatever you want."

"Great." He clapped and jumped from the car. As she exited the passenger side, he ran up the entrance steps, unlocked the door, and held it open for her. "After you, beautiful."

Without hesitation, she crossed the threshold, as he dialed a number on his cell phone and ordered a pepperoni pizza. The grandfather clock chimed the hour, as she hung her gown in the entry closet.

"What do you want to watch?" Scanning the titles on a bookshelf, all of which were on VCR tape, she laughed. "Not many choices,

85

because Minnie's got nothing prior to nineteen ninety."

"Does that surprise you?" At the fireplace, he stacked some logs, struck a match, and tossed it atop a small mound of kindling. "And dinner is on its way."

He was nothing if not efficient when he was horny, and she recalled the smooth talk he used to lure her into his car, in the tavern parking lot.

"How about *Poltergeist?*" The story of an innocent family haunted by a dark secret from the past seemed appropriate. "The original one."

How stupid she'd been, as a girl. Yet, it seemed she hadn't wised up enough to avoid the same fate. But this time she looked at him with her eyes wide open.

"Sure." He strolled into the kitchen and returned with some paper plates, two forks, napkins, and a couple of beers. On the coffee table, he pushed aside the crocheted doily, picked up the remote, and turned on the television. "Sit down, baby."

After shoving the boxy tape into the VCR, she plopped beside him and braced herself. Everything inside her focused on her sole objective, on getting even, and it didn't take long for him to assert his goal, because he was on her before the opening credits played.

Pinning her beneath his strong, muscled body, he pressed his hips to hers, making it clear he wanted her as she wanted him, although she suspected their motives differed. In rhythm with his thrusts, he plunged his tongue into her mouth, and she grasped fistfuls of his thick brown hair.

Hunger blossomed in the pit of her belly, and she experienced the same sensation on graduation night. The ignorant virgin wanted him. Older and smarter, she wanted him to know he hurt her, and she wanted him to feel the same pain. To know the ache. The emptiness.

When he unbuttoned her shirt, shoved her bra out of the way, and sucked hard on her nipple, she cried out, as heat speared through her. The next thing she knew, he'd inched her jeans to her knees and slipped his hand inside her panties.

The doorbell rang.

"Damn." Russ backed off her and wiped his mouth. "Don't get dressed, because I'll be just a second."

"All right." Cool and calm, she reached behind her and unhooked her bra, from which she tugged free and tossed on the floor. Then she stripped from her jeans and prepared to attack.

When he returned, holding a pizza box, she claimed the advantage and unbuttoned and unzipped his jeans. Remembering what he taught her, as they crouched in the backseat of the Camaro, when he held her head down, as he shoved his dick in her mouth, she locked her lips around his erection, licked the mushroom tip, and he groaned.

"No, Cindy." To her shock, he retreated, set the pizza on the table, and grabbed her wrists. "Not here, and not like this."

"Why not? What's wrong?" They wrestled until he eased to the couch, and she wondered why he fought her, because he sure as hell didn't three years ago. Despite his weird reaction to her aggression, his hard dick pointed straight at her. "This was your idea."

"I know, but I want to do it right." As he tried to brush her off, she pressed his palm to her bare breast, and he relented. Seizing the edge, she straddled him, yanked aside her undies, and lowered herself over him. As she joined their bodies and rode him, he sucked in a breath and dug his fingernails into her ass. "Because I want to make you forget all the others, especially the last guy."

Knife to the gut, and she halted her movements. "You are the last guy."

"What?" In that moment, he framed her face. "What are you saying?"

"You're the last, Russ." And it killed her to admit it.

"You mean, you've never been with anyone else, in three years?" He blinked. "No one?"

Cindy shook her head. "No, I haven't."

"Boy, I did a real number on you." For a few minutes, he just stared at her. "But you still want me. You really want me." Then he stood, taking her with him, cradled her in his arms, and carried her down the hall, to his room. After kicking the door shut, he eased to the bed. "We'll eat later."

CHAPTER FIVE

Sunlight peeked through the drapes, as Russ rolled onto his back and rubbed his wicked erection, driven by images of last night. With a smile, he reached for Cindy's warm and soft body but grasped nothing but a cold pillow. Stretching his arms overhead, he opened his eyes and discovered he was alone.

"Cindy?" he called.

A glance at the clock told him Granny Minnie was home, so he cursed under his breath, threw aside the covers, sifted through his clothes, and pulled on his sweatpants. Shirtless and barefooted, he opened the door to his room, peered into the hallway, and then crept, the wood floor creaking beneath his steps, into the kitchen.

"Cindy, are you there?"

To his surprise and confusion, she was

A TASTE OF MAGICK

gone.

In the living room, he noticed she'd taken her phone, and his remained on the coffee table, where he'd left it, before they took to his bed, and he fucked—no, he made love to her three times before dawn. And as Rafe rightly asserted, there was a definite difference.

As he sat on the couch, which he'd never look at the same again, because that's where everything started, Cindy's sweet moans and muffled cries filled his ears, and he recalled how she clung to him as he took her. How she wrapped her legs about him and dug her heels into his ass, urging him to go faster. The way she kissed him, as he rested between her thighs. And her gentle touch, as she framed his face and held his stare, while he plunged his dick deep within her.

So why did she leave without even saying goodbye?

When he checked his phone, he found no texts from her, explaining her absence. He walked onto the porch, glanced at her house, and noticed her bike was gone. In some respects, it was as though she'd laid and left him, but little Miss Parker would never do that to him.

Or would she?

As he typed a quick greeting, something occurred to him, and he deleted the message. When he stepped into the foyer, the grandfather clock counted down the seconds, and Russ inhaled a deep breath. Closing his eyes, he centered himself, shut out the world, opened the door to his memory, and revisited what happened, yesterday, because his instincts told him that he missed something.

While he hated his ability, it had its benefits.

Searching through the various fragments of their exchange, he pieced together a startling vision and seized on a dark presence, hiding in the margins of her inner dialogue. A deep-seated desire, stealthy and elusive, as it danced on the fringe of Cindy's passion, disguised itself as nothing more than healthy enthusiasm for him, but nothing could have been further from the ugly truth.

A strange sensation danced along his spine, mocking him, and he shuddered, as realization dawned.

She didn't want him.

"She wanted revenge," he said, to no one.

Somehow, giving voice to the simple awareness made it seem that much worse, and he leaned forward and cradled his head in his hands.

"So that's how it feels."

Of course, he corrected himself, because, although Cindy screwed him, and she'd certainly wounded him, she didn't call him a whore to her friends. No, that was his game.

"I deserved this."

Still, that elementary statement, and the fact that he agreed with it, did nothing to ease the knot in his stomach or the ache in his chest. Before he ran amok and scared Minnie, he showered, shaved, dressed, grabbed his keys, and drove to the tavern, where he just might find some peace.

"Hey, boss two, what are you doing here?" At the range, Tony stirred a pan of gravy and tossed in a handful of flour. "You don't work on Sundays, not that you ever really work, but that's beside the point."

"Tony, I swear, everyone who ever loved you was wrong." That's what Russ needed just then. A good insult. "How you tricked Clover into marrying you is going to go down as one of life's greatest mysteries."

"That's right, because I have neither the time nor the crayons to explain it to you, little man." With a snicker, Tony poured heavy cream into the skillet. "But all you need to know is Mrs. Deluca loves me, and she's lucky, because I'm a catch."

"Oh, yeah?" Russ laughed. "Hey, I'm just curious, did your mother have any kids that lived?"

"Not bad, boss two." Tony lowered his chin. "Especially for a guy whose birth certificate is an apology letter from a condom factory. Now, why don't you go into the office, before someone drops a house on you."

Russ squared his shoulders. "Tony, if I was your wife, I'd poison your beer."

"Kid, if you were my wife, I'd drink it." The cook grinned. "Because you have all the sex appeal of a camel with gingivitis."

"Damn, that's good." Russ slapped his thigh. "Let me guess, you learned human as a second language."

"Hey, that was sharp." Tony snorted and then narrowed his stare. "Suppose you stop fiddle-farting around, and tell me what's wrong. Why are you here?"

"Is it that obvious?" Russ asked.

"Yep." Tony shook his head. "You're moping so bad you remind me of Bark Twain, my old basset hound. What'd you do, have a fight with Cindy?"

"Why do you think it involves her?" Russ shuffled his feet. "Could've been anyone."

"Because you're not crazy about just

anyone." Sprinkling salt in the pan, Tony chuckled. "You are grade A, prime time in love with Cindy Parker, and it appears everyone knows it but you. Maybe that's your problem, although I'd argue you've got several others, and she's the least of them."

"I wish it were that simple." And Russ couldn't elaborate without causing Cindy further embarrassment.

"Look, it don't take a genius to know the solution." Tony peered over his shoulder. "All you got to do is apologize. Trust me, whenever I get on the wrong side of Clover, and that's few and far between, because I'm an angel, I tell her I'm sorry, and that's that. Believe me, whatever you did, she'll forgive you, because women are made that way. I read somewhere that they were born with an extra understanding gene or some sort, which makes sense, because they put up with us."

"Do you really believe the shit you're spewing?" For a few minutes, Russ forgot his troubles and relaxed. In that brief instant of clarity, he gained some perspective. "What if I did something, a long time ago, and I hurt Cindy? Then, when I came home, I tried to make it up to her, and I thought she forgave me, but I found out she didn't."

"And she fought back?" Leaning against

the counter, Tony wrinkled his nose, when Russ nodded. "That ain't like her, so I'd be asking myself what set her off, because she's a sweetheart, and she wouldn't harm a flea."

"I know, but she...well, she took a shot, and I got hit pretty bad." Hell, she brought him to his knees. "But she didn't do half of what I did to her."

"Can you cut it up with me?" Tony wiped his hands on his apron.

"Not without causing her more humiliation, and I'd sever my left nut before I did that." Russ winced at the mere suggestion. "But I'll just say that what she did was justified. It was provoked."

"Then give her some time." Tony grabbed a bowl of eggs from the fridge. "If she did what you say, her conscience will eat at her, and she'll come back to you, if you let her."

"How can you be sure?" Russ desperately wanted to believe his friend.

"Because I know her." Tony shrugged. "And consider yourself, because you know what you did. How do you feel about hurting her?"

"It happened three years ago, and it still kills me." Russ could only imagine what it did to her. "But I thought we'd made some headway, since I came home, and I was planning for our future."

"Whoa." Mid-stir, Tony halted. "You're that serious about her?"

"Yeah, I am. I think I've always been serious about Cindy." Now, Russ prayed she'd give him a chance. "I just don't understand what went wrong, because everything was going fine, until last night."

"Okay, start from there." With no fanfare, Tony snatched a cutting board from a wall peg and pulled a knife from the butcher block. "What were you doing?"

Shit. No way could Russ share that information. Then he realized Tony was on to something. "I met her at the dry cleaners."

"Was that unusual?" Without missing a beat, and with lethal precision, Tony diced two onions. "I thought she was working on the bakery."

"She picked up a dress for the Samhain Ball." In that instant, Russ jolted to the past. To the parking lot behind the tavern. The conversation, still painful to recall, came to him, word for word.

I've never been to one of the wild parties. And I never would've imagined going with the most popular guy in school.

Yeah, about that. Look, it's mainly my crew, and you'd be bored, so why don't you go home?

97

You don't want to be seen with me? Are you ashamed of me? Are you afraid of what your friends will think?

Of course, Cindy was right.

"Is it really that obvious?" Russ rubbed the back of his neck. "She wanted to go to the party, and she even bought a gown for the event, but I wanted to stay home."

Tony whistled in monotone. "Don't you know that anytime a woman buys new clothes that it's serious? I mean, you got to go whole hog, with fancy flowers and an expensive dinner." The cook frowned. "I once made the mistake of taking Clover to the burger joint on the highway, before the ball, because she wouldn't make up her mind where she wanted to eat, so I made the decision, and I will never hear the end of it. It'll probably be written into my obituary."

"It's not that simple." Russ cursed himself a fool. "This goes deep, and I should have known better." Smacking a fist to a palm, he kicked a trashcan. "Dammit, I hurt her, again, when that was not my intention, but she thinks I didn't want to be seen with her. She thinks I'm ashamed of her."

"Why would she even—never mind." Tony splayed his palms. "Well, you need to show her otherwise, don't you?"

"Yeah, I do." Despite what happened, Russ wasn't mad at her, but he was angry with himself, because she was so disappointed when he asked her to stay at Minnie's. He should have recognized and read her desires, but he'd been too selfish and preoccupied with what he wanted. "And I think I know just where to begin." He saluted the cook. "Thanks, Tony."

"Any time, boss two."

In the office, Russ flipped through a few stacks of papers and then rummaged through a couple of drawers, until he found what he sought. Smiling, he toyed with the ruffled edge of Cindy's copy of the restaurant supply catalogue.

At the computer, he opened his email and clicked on a particular contact.

To: Leonard@Grangerrestaurantsupply.com
Subject: Sweet & Spooky Bakery

Lenny,
Per our phone conversation last week, I'd like to purchase the items we discussed, and I need them delivered to the bakery, at the address I provided. Please check your inventory, ship everything ASAP, and bill the tavern account.
Thank you.

Russell Lee McBride
The Old Haven Mill Tavern

~

Until recently, regret had been an unfamiliar emotion that plagued other people, those who had no clear understanding of themselves or lacked the strength to fight for what they wanted, and they deserved what they got. At least, that's what Cindy thought, prior to her split with Russell.

Ignorance was truly bliss.

In the wake of the one-night-stand with the man she had long viewed as her tormentor, when she screwed him and left him cold, she learned just how wrong she'd been, because she knew exactly who she was, and she worked hard for everything she had. Still, remorse devoured her conscience, haunting her every waking moment and terrorizing her dreams, because she'd deliberately set out to hurt Russ. Just that once, she wished she'd failed, but it appeared she'd been successful in her endeavor, because she hadn't heard a peep from him.

Yet she celebrated no victory.

While she expected some sense of satisfaction after giving him a dose of his own medicine, she never anticipated the guilt that gnawed at her gut. In the two days since that fateful night, she'd hardly slept or eaten, because she hated what she did to him, and she reserved a harsh description, which she couldn't repeat aloud, for herself.

In fact, she was so ashamed she couldn't face him, and she resorted to baking her goods in her kitchen. Before dawn, Tony stopped by and picked up the items to sell at the tavern. In those torturous hours, if Russ suffered half as much as she did, he'd suffered enough.

"Cindy Louise Parker, you have to apologize."

Sitting on her ankles, she dropped her sponge into a bucket, wiped her brow, fished her phone from her jeans pocket, and for the umpteenth time considered texting him. Just as fast, she stopped herself.

"If he wanted to talk to me, he would've called."

Standing, she dusted herself and sighed. Whether or not she wanted to admit it, what she did to him was wrong. No matter what he did to her, she had no right to compound the pain surrounding his actions, three years ago, by striking at him. By intentionally wounding him.

"Then again, I'm the one who hurt him, this time. It's up to me to make the first move and beg forgiveness, and I need to do it in person."

Without hesitation, she dialed a familiar number.

"The Old Haven Mill Tavern, this is Tony."

"Hey, Tony." Suddenly shaking, she inhaled a deep breath and prayed for calm, but her voice quivered as she asked, "How'd the lunch rush go?"

"Miss Parker, always good to hear you on the other end." He chuckled. "As usual, all your stuff is sold out, and I've got a stack of orders, including two birthday cakes, for tomorrow."

"Wow. That's great." Shuffling her feet, she shifted her weight and reminded herself that she was no coward. She knew what she did, and she had to own it. "I was wondering if Russ was there."

"No, he's not, little lady. He went home, early."

"Is everything all right?" Anxious, she bit her lip, because Russ never missed the dinner crowd. "He's not sick is he?"

"Naw, he's fit as a fiddle, so don't you worry your pretty head. But he's been pulling some long hours, and he looked like the walking dead, so I told him to skedaddle."

"Oh, okay." She knew about long hours, as well as the reason behind them, and her regret intensified. If she had to crawl on her hands and knees, she'd do it to win Russ back. There would always be another Samhain Ball, but there was only one Russell Lee McBride, and she loved him. "Well, if you'll email the orders, I'll have everything ready, in the morning."

"Sounds like a plan, kiddo. You take care."

"You, too." Just as she ended the call, someone pounded at the front door, and she peered into the shop. Beyond the glass, a deliveryman waved. "Just a second."

As she ran to the door, she pulled the keys from her pocket and then unlocked the bolt.

"Hi." The guy scanned a couple of boxes with a handheld device. "I've got some packages for Cindy Parker."

"That would be me." She laughed and signed for the items. "Just put them here."

He did as she asked. "There you go. Have a good day."

"You, too." As soon as he departed, she grabbed an X-acto knife from the counter and slit the packing tape. Inside the parcel, she found the custom printed tablecloths she wanted but couldn't yet afford to purchase. "Wait a minute. I didn't buy these."

The other boxes yielded the delicate china, with her store name, and the silverware that she coveted but also opted to forgo, along with matching paper plates and plastic utensils, for to-go orders. As she searched for the shipping receipt, another man appeared at the door.

"Yes, can I help you?" she asked.

"I'm here to install your awning, the matching valances, and the sign." He smiled. "Is it okay if I set up my ladder, here?"

She blinked.

"Uh—there must be some mistake, because I didn't order an awning or a sign, much less valances." Low on funds, because the setup cost more than she anticipated, she decided to use white shoe polish to write the business name on the windows. Yeah, it was low-tech, but it was cheap.

"Nope, there's no mistake." He handed her a clipboard and pointed to the details. "Says right there that a Russell McBride paid for them, and the price included installation."

"I see that." And she realized much more, in that instant. Had she thought she wrestled with guilt? It burned a hole right through her gut. "Then I'll get out of your way, but can you let me know when you're done?"

"Yes, ma'am." He nodded once.

As she strolled to the center of her bakery, tears welled, but she didn't have a chance to cry, because another knock at the door had her glancing over her shoulder, only to spy yet another deliveryman.

"Russell Lee, what have you done, now?" Rolling her shoulders, she summoned calm as she greeted the stranger. "Yes? What can I do for you?"

"I'm from Granger Restaurant Supply." Oh, no. Narrowing his stare, he adjusted his glasses and read from a cluster of documents. "Are you Cindy Parker?"

"Yes, sir. The one and only." She braced, as he handed her the requisite papers. "I'm guessing you have a delivery for me?"

"Yes, ma'am. How about I have my guys put your boxes by the counter?" Resting fists on hips, he surveyed the dining area. "Then we'll unpack your tables and chairs and bring them inside, so we can recycle the wrapping, unless you have use for all that."

"No, that sounds great." Actually, it sounded awful, in the wake of what she did to Russ. Retreating, she bowed her head, because she was going to cry, and it wasn't going to be one of those silent weeping fits. Oh, no. It was going to be one of those ugly, heaving, teeth-gnashing, wail jobs. "Thank you."

Turning on a heel, Cindy clenched her jaw and then sprinted to her office, where she slammed shut the door, leaned her back to the wall, and then slid to the floor, where she hugged her knees to her chest and unleashed an emotional tidal wave. Sobbing, she gasped for air, as she clung to her ankles, and it felt so good to release the tension that had coiled in the pit of her belly, since Saturday.

Bawling like a baby, she reminisced of everything that passed between her and Russell, and she knew what she had to do, one way or another. First, she needed to know the truth behind his generosity, or she was done with him, because if he couldn't talk to her, there was nothing left for them. Second, he had to know she loved him, and she vowed to endure his acceptance or rejection of her devotion.

After several minutes of knockdown, drag-out howling in misery, she crawled to her new desk, grasped the edge, and stood. In the process, she knocked over a file stand, and the bank papers scattered. As she collected the documents, she noted the name of the financial group that backed her loan, and a chill of unease danced a jig along her spine. She didn't know why she did it, but she opened a browser on her phone and searched for 2M Capital Group. It was as though the company didn't exist, because there wasn't a single entry—not even a website.

"Two-M Capital Group." Her words echoed in her brain, and then she flinched. "McBride. Russell Lee and Mary-George McBride. Two-M." Dropping back her head, she focused on the ceiling. "What have I done?"

In a flurry of activity, she read and reread the information, and she could find no mention of the government grant that supposedly covered her rent for a year. How had she missed that?

Her knees buckled, as she stumbled into the bathroom, and she splashed cold water on her face. Exhausted from a severe bout of sleep deprivation, a state of near-starvation, and a lack of the energy she spent on a good cry, she wiped her brow with a towel and returned to the bakery dining area.

As the men carried in the very tables and chairs she'd shown Russ, something occurred to her, and she recalled she'd given him the catalogue of wishes. Never had she imagined that, when he asked to borrow her collection of dreams, he would purchase everything she'd marked.

It was then she gave her attention to the boxes on the counter. In one, she located gorgeous crystal bud vases, for fresh flowers, when she'd planned to use paper cups, to save money. In the other, she discovered unique napkin holders in bright red with lace scrollwork, which complimented the rich beige walls, upon which she'd hung framed posters from past Witches Walks, the single accent wall in red, at the back, and the white trim. It was a lovely touch that she had missed, but nothing escaped Russ.

"Miss Parker, we're all done." The delivery guy dusted his hands. "What do you think?"

"It's beautiful." Caressing the back of a white chair, one of many, she admired a round table and swallowed a sob. "Thank you."

"Then we'll get out of your hair." He nodded. "Have a good evening, ma'am."

"You, too." As she walked him to the door, the other guy waved, and she stepped outside. "Yes? Is there something I can do for you?"

"You tell me." He pointed. "How does it look?"

Rotating, Cindy savored the first glimpse of her vision, and it was more stunning than she expected, and only one thing was missing.

Russ.

The black and white awning contrasted perfectly with the red brick façade, and the coordinating valances in the front windows completed the fantasy. But it was the stained and varnished hand-carved sign, proudly displaying *Sweet & Spooky Bakery*, which hung from a wrought-iron bracket, that again brought tears to her eyes.

"I don't know what to say." She sniffed. "Other than thank you."

"Hey, I'd eat here." He laughed. "When do you open?"

"Monday, November twentieth, the week of Thanksgiving." Swallowing hard, she squared her shoulders. "But I'm holding a soft opening on Friday, the seventeenth, if you'd like to drop by, and try something for free."

"I'll tell my wife." He closed and picked up his ladder. "Well, if that's all, I'll be going."

Thunder rumbled overhead, as she gazed at the cloudy sky, and the wind whipped and howled, heralding an approaching storm. Checking her watch, she noted the time and doubted anyone would miss her, if she closed for the day, because she needed to get to Minnie's.

After securing the bakery, she hopped on

her bike. Raindrops dotted the pavement, as she sped down Oak Street, and she pedaled faster toward a date with destiny.

CHAPTER SIX

The house rattled, as lightning flashed, and the skies opened, as Russ switched on a lamp. At the window, he peered into the deluge, thought of Cindy, and worried about her safety, given the torrential sheets of rain. Against his better judgment, he opened the messaging app on his phone, to offer her a ride, but he feared he might only push her further away, and they'd already been apart way too long for his liking. To his shock, in that instant, she rolled up on her bike, stopping on the path, just short of the stairs, and he rushed onto the porch.

"Hey." Could he not have thought of something better to say? Given the storm, he waved. "Come inside, before you get soaked and catch a cold."

"I'm already soaked." Like some valiant storybook heroine, supremely confident in her position, she thrust her chin, and how he admired her invincible spirit. Because, despite her disadvantages, which were not of her making, she persevered. Hell, she thrived. "Why did you do it?"

Ah, the shipments must've arrived.

It was as if every moment in his life had prepared him for that confrontation, yet his courage faltered, because so much weighed in the balance, and it was one battle he had to win.

"Because you wanted it." A tangled mass of emotion, none of which he could decipher, caught him in a relentless grip, and he stiffened his spine, to withstand the onslaught. Yet her torment threatened to rip him in two. "I took everything from your catalogue, and I threw in a few things you forgot, because I want you to have your dream, and I'm in a position to give it to you." He shrugged. "You deserve it. Isn't that reason enough?"

"*No.*" To his surprise, she flung her ten-speed into the grass, squared her shoulders, and clenched her fists. God, she was glorious. "Tell me the truth, Russell Lee, or, so help me, I'm going to sell everything—the bakery and my house, and I'll move as far from here

as I can get, because I can't live like this."
Then she broke, clutched her throat, and
sobbed, and an unforgivable wave of agony
twisted his insides. "I can't eat. I can't sleep.
I can't stop thinking about you and what I
did. It's killing me, Russ. It's killing me, and I
need to know the truth. Why did you do it?
Why did you help me, after I deliberately hurt
you?"

In that instant, he realized she meant more
than the material goods he purchased, and he
owed her an honest answer, when his senses
zeroed in on a startling revelation she couldn't
hide from him if she tried. Suddenly,
everything became clear, and he stood his
ground in equal measure.

"Because I love you." He vented a self-
mocking snort, because it didn't kill him to
admit. "Because I think I've loved you since
we were in the second grade, and you
defended me against that bully, Jimmy Doyle,
by kicking him in the shins, during recess.
And I could invent all sorts of excuses to
explain why I bought that stuff, but the
reason is because I love you." He splayed his
palms. "I love you, Cindy Parker."

With a strange, throaty wail, she broke into
a sprint, ran up the stairs, and launched
herself at him, and he caught her, mid-air.

Clinging to him, she buried her face in the curve of his neck and cried, and he rocked her, back and forth. As the wind whistled and howled, she shivered, so he carried her into the house, where he simply held her.

"Shh." He rubbed her back. "It's okay, baby. We're okay, I promise."

"No, we're not." Shifting, she met his stare, and what he spied in her blue eyes wrenched his heart. "I'm so sorry I left you, and I hate myself for it, but I'll make it up to you, I swear, because I love you, too."

That had to have been the sweetest confession, ever.

"Honey, I know why you did it, and I'm to blame, because I should have told you why I didn't want to go to the ball." When she shuddered, he frowned and continued to his bedroom, where he eased her to the mattress. "First, let's get you out of those wet clothes, before you catch your death, and I'll explain everything."

From the bathroom, Russell fetched a towel, and as she dried her hair and face, he grabbed a pair of sweats from the closet. As she peeled out of her drenched shirt and bra, he stared at the floor. But when she shimmied from her jeans and undies, he knelt, kissed her knees, and held the sweat bottoms for her. After tugging on a pair of his socks, Cindy stood, and the sweats dropped to her ankles.

Together, they burst into laughter.

"I don't think this is going to work." She pouted, and everything emanating from her told him she just wanted to be held. "And I'm cold."

"Here." He yanked back the comforter, sat, and slapped his thighs. As he expected, she settled in his lap, and he tucked the covers about her. "Better?"

"Much." Resting her head to his chest, she hugged him about the waist and closed her eyes, and her inner dialogue all but screamed she loved him—not that he doubted it. Yet, once again, along the fringes lurked something dark and painful, and it was time to address her long-held fears, which he caused.

"Baby, the reason I didn't want to attend the Samhain Ball had nothing to do with you." In his arms, she tensed. "I would've been proud to take you, for all to see, but I didn't go, because I'm one of *them*."

"Them?" With a gentle nuzzle, she nipped his chin. "What do you mean?"

It was now or never.

"I have powers. I was born with them." He could only pray she didn't run away, when she discovered the whole ugly truth about him, but her rejection would destroy him. Still, he couldn't hide, forever. As Mary-George reminded him, she almost lost Rafe because she lied to him about her ability, and Russ wasn't about to make the same mistake. "The technical term is claircognizance of desire, but it simply means I know what people want. I can read them—their thoughts, like a book."

"Okay."

He waited for some sign of disgust or panic. Instead, she just burrowed closer, as nature beat a steady rhythm on the roof, which seemed to match the hammering of his heart. The clock on the nightstand ticked off the seconds, and thunder roared, but she remained silent.

"Did you hear what I just said?" He held his breath and tried to interpret her response, but his emotions functioned as a barrier, blocking his capacity to gain any insight.

"Mmm hmm." She nodded but made no attempt to break free. "Apparently, you have the same gift as Mary-George."

"Wait a minute." Cupping her chin, he brought her gaze to his. "You know about my sister?"

"Yep." She brushed her lips to his, and a

vicious hunger erupted and reverberated from within her. "I've worked, side by side, with her, since I was sixteen. Did you really think I wouldn't notice her ability to guess the bar patrons' drink choices was grounded in something more than luck? Really, Russ, I'm not that naïve, and she never got it wrong. No one's that accurate without some sort of power."

"Why didn't you tell me you knew?" Beneath the blankets, he gripped her bare ass, and goose bumps covered her flesh.

"Why would I?" Adjusting her weight, she straddled him. "It was her business, not mine." Then she rested her forehead to his. "I missed you. Everything is coming together at the bakery, and I should be thrilled, but I'm miserable, because I want to share it with you."

And she wanted him, but he needed no magick to get that.

"I missed you, too." In that moment, he bent his head, and they exchanged a thorough kiss. "I should have told you a long time ago, but there are a lot of things I should've done, and no one knew of my skill—not even Mary-George, until recently. And I never told my parents."

"Then why didn't you take me to the ball?"

Yeah, that still hurt her. "What did it have to do with your ability, because I fail to see the relationship?"

"Because I don't want to be a witch, I thought I could escape my birthright by avoiding their company." At her expression of confusion, he caressed her cheek. "Look, I know it sounds stupid, but I never claimed to be a genius. And I wanted you to myself, because I'm greedy where you're concerned. Given the choice, I'd rather spend an evening in front of the television, watching corny old movies, than go to some fancy party and hang with the coven."

"I assumed you were ashamed of me," she said, in a small voice. "Like you were on graduation night."

"Oh, baby, that was not my best moment, was it?" Overflowing with anguish, she scooted closer and teased his erection, and he ached to make love to her. He would do so, soon, but he needed to resolve their differences, first. "If I was half the man I thought I was, I'd have told my so-called friends to go fuck themselves. Instead, I caved, and I lost the most important person in my world. I know I have no right to ask, but can you ever forgive me?"

"You never lost me, Russ, but I think you

lost your way." She swept aside the hair from his face. "And I forgave you that night, so don't be so hard on yourself, because you were just a kid, and you're a better man than you realize. I mean, who else would expend so much effort to help me launch my bakery?" She teased his nose with hers. "Don't deny it, or I'll be pissed. When did you form Two-M Capital Group? And am I really the beneficiary of some mysterious federal neighborhood revitalization grant, or did the Russell Lee McBride charitable fund ride to my rescue?"

Busted.

"It's not charity, and you'll pay me back." His mind raced, as he searched for an explanation for the remainder of his scheme. In the end, he settled for honesty. "As for the company, it was a spur of the moment venture, and George and I plan to fund other projects, in town. And it just so happens I own that block, with my sister, and I can charge whatever rent I want. Plus, you're a good investment." Again, he squeezed her. "Besides, you've got other *ass*ets that I value much more than money."

"Is that so?" She trailed a finger along the crest of his ear. Yep, she flirted with him.

"Yeah." Damn, he struggled not to jump

her.

"When does Minnie get home?" Now, she was speaking his language, as she wiggled her hips and teased his dick. "How much time do we have before we're interrupted?"

"Later tonight." Just as quick, her desire waned, much to his disappointment. "But we have a few hours."

"No, that won't do." When Cindy pulled free, his heart plummeted, because her behavior conflicted with her passion, and he grasped at any excuse to make her stay. Collecting her clothes, she glanced over her shoulder and winked. "Pack whatever you need, for the night and work, tomorrow, and let's go to my place, where we won't be interrupted."

"Are you serious?" When she nodded, he could have cried. In that instant, Russ grinned and leaped from the bed. "Baby, you don't have to ask me twice."

~

It was still dark, on the day of the soft opening, when Cindy woke to the distinct odor of something burning. Jolting upright, she reached for Russ and discovered him gone. In a panic, she flipped on the lamp, jumped from her warm bed, shrugged into her robe, and ran downstairs. Just as she sprinted into the kitchen, the fire alarm blared.

"Dammit." Standing on a step-stool, Russ yanked the battery from the unit and silenced the ear-piercing tone.

On the stove, smoke billowed from a skillet of bacon she could've carbon dated, given he'd all but reduced it to ash. In another pan, scorched eggs had her gagging, and she choked. After switching off the gas, she grabbed a towel, removed both disasters to the sink, and turned on the faucet.

"Honey, what are you doing?" After opening the window, she unlocked and pushed wide the side door, to let in fresh air. "Are you trying to set fire to the house?"

In the weeks since they reconciled, he spent every night with her, and there was nothing like going to sleep and waking in his arms. While their days were occupied with final preparations for the bakery's grand opening, the wee hours had become a time for exploration and discovery, and oh, what they discovered.

"Aw, babe, what are you doing up?" As he stowed the step-stool, he frowned. "I wanted to surprise you."

"Trust me, you did." Broken shells and raw egg littered the counter, and she picked up an uncooked strip of bacon from the floor.

Then she noted the empty tin and peered into the oven. "Um, sweetheart, you have to turn on the heat if you want to bake something."

"Are you kidding? I'm an idiot." He smacked his forehead, as she grabbed the sponge. "I wanted to fix your breakfast, like Rafe does for George, to celebrate your special day, and I made a mess. I'm sorry."

"Don't be, because it's the thought that counts, and Rafe knows how to cook, whereas you're still learning." From the fridge, she gathered the carton of eggs and the package of bacon. After pulling out the pan of cinnamon rolls, she set the oven to preheat. "And I should be treating you, after that lovely meal at The Judges Chambers, last night." Indeed, it was a memorable evening, and they got all dressed up for the candlelit dinner he arranged. Then he brought her home, stripped her naked, and made love to her until she screamed. "Tell you what, why don't we do it, together, and I'll walk you through the process?"

"Okay." His adorable pout melted her heart, but then he brightened. "Hey, at least, I got the coffee right." When he glanced at the empty carafe, his grin faltered. "Wait—what happened? How could I screw that up, when all I had to do was throw in the grounds and flip a switch?"

"Let me check." A brief search provided the answer. "Uh, sweetie, you have to put water in the reservoir, and you should fill it to the top line."

"I'm a failure." He shook his head. "I don't know why you love me."

Of course, he was joking, and she knew his ploy, which she would humor.

"Poor baby. And I'd tell you why I love you, but there are countless reasons, and we've got to get to the bakery. So, how about I show you?" After lining up fresh strips of bacon in a clean skillet, she turned on the gas, on low, just as the oven pinged. At the center of the rack, she placed the pan of cinnamon rolls and closed the door. Then she consoled her man. "Come here, because I haven't had my good morning kiss."

Without hesitation, he walked into her waiting embrace. "Now, that I can do."

"And you do it so very well." When he waggled his brows, she giggled, until he bent his head, grabbed her ass, and pressed his lips to hers. Ah, that never got old, but before things got out of hand, and with him that was a safe bet, she halted his play. "That's much better, and I should scramble the eggs. Why don't you turn the bacon?"

"I'm on it." With a pair of metal tongs, he did as she asked. "Hey, this looks pretty good, and the fat isn't popping."

"If you use lower heat, the bacon cooks evenly, too." To the eggs, she added salt and pepper, as well as grated cheese. The timer on the oven buzzed, and she pulled out the rolls, which had browned to perfection. "Feast your eyes on these beauties."

"You know, I didn't realize just how hard it is to do what you do." From a cupboard, he collected two plates, drew a couple of forks from a drawer, and then poured two mugs of coffee. "I thought I could just throw some food on the stove, and magic would happen."

"Well, there's a little more to it than that." At the table, she dished the eggs, added the bacon, and then iced the cinnamon rolls. "But you have talent in other more important areas." She stuck her tongue in her cheek, as she pinched his cute ass. Since the smoke had dissipated, she closed the door and the window and clicked on the heater. "I missed you when I woke up, because I'm used to you being there."

"How about we grab a quickie in the shower, because we've got to bust a move." He glanced at the clock. "And in the interest of time, I'll scrub your back."

A TASTE OF MAGICK

"Sounds like a plan." Cindy snickered. "And I'm grateful for your sacrifice. Now, take a seat, because we're ready to eat."

After a lovely breakfast, during which Russ fed her bites of cinnamon rolls with his own hands, he did exactly as he promised. An hour later, as light snow fell, they hopped into the Camaro and drove to the bakery, where they shifted into overdrive.

Working in concert, they filled the cases with a huge assortment of delicate pastries, cookies, *petit fours*, cupcakes, pies, and cakes. By the time she flipped the switch on the commercial coffeemaker, a crowd lingered on the sidewalk.

"Well, this is it." He enveloped her in his strong embrace and kissed her forehead. "I'm so proud of you."

"But this is your achievement just as much as it is mine, and I'm proud of *us*." In light of everything he'd given her, there was something she wanted to do for him. "Before everything gets crazy, I was thinking about the Camaro. I know you want to sell it, but you're not sure what you'll use until you get something else. I want you to have the Charger."

"Baby, as much as I love that car, it was your grandfather's pride and joy." Despite his

125

tempered response, his expression conveyed just how excited he was by the prospect. And the lone afternoon she let him take her for a spin in the Dodge, he made love to her for three hours, after they got home, and she wondered what he'd do for an encore. "It's a generous gift, but I can't accept it, because he left it to his family."

"And he'd want it to go to someone who values it, just as much as he did." She cupped his cheek. "He'd want to see it driven and enjoyed, instead of gathering dust in the garage. And after all you've given me, you've more than earned it."

"You know, I can modify the engine, to get better gas mileage." Russ licked his lips. "Everything else is in prime condition, just like my woman."

"Then consider it yours." On tiptoes, she kissed him with a loud smack. "Okay, it's now or never, sink or swim."

"Go to it, baby." Russ slapped her ass. "I've got your back, but you're gonna be great."

Although it was a short walk to the front entrance, it seemed to stretch for miles, as Cindy navigated the sea of little white tables and chairs. Beyond the glass, Mary-George, Rafe, Tony, Clover, and so many friends from

A TASTE OF MAGICK

the tavern waited. After she flipped the antique sign to *Open*, she unlocked the bolt and set wide the door. "Welcome to the Sweet & Spooky Bakery."

EPILOGUE

October, 2018

At a long table, five of Haven Harbor's most prominent citizens displayed their best poker face, as they scribbled on small slips of paper, which they handed to the master of ceremonies. It was a longstanding tradition, which heralded the holiday season and crowned the queen of country culinary cuisine. The crowd held its collective breath, as everyone anticipated the winner of the annual Spooktacular Fang-tastic Cast-iron Cauldron Cook-off, the premier event at the Haven County Fair.

To the left, the four finalists, Minnie, Lometa Adams, granny's chief rival, Hazel Jandrucko, and a newcomer, Cindy Parker,

Haven Harbor's rising star, awaited the announcement.

"Oh, I wish they'd hurry, because I'm about to bust." Mary-George, pregnant with her second child, bounced and squeezed Rafe's hand, as Russ cradled his nephew. "While I love Minnie, and she's family, Cindy's entry was the best, by far."

"I couldn't agree more." Tony snorted. "Maybe because I taught her everything she knows."

"And you're so modest," Clover replied.

In the year since Russ moved in with Cindy, so much had happened. The bakery was a huge success, and that summer they partnered with the tavern, which ventured into catering, and doubled their business. In June, they celebrated her graduation from UMass, and a week later, they did the same at his commencement, in Boston. And Easton Robb, an eighty-year-old marathon runner and a retired railroad engineer, mentored Russ, so he could learn to accept and manage his gift. While he was no expert, he was getting there.

Tonight marked the beginning of the next chapter in his life, and he'd already set his plan in motion. Regardless of the contest outcome, Minnie had a gift to present to

Cindy, in front of everyone, and he'd argue she'd claimed the bigger prize.

"Ladies and gentlemen, I am pleased to declare the winner of this year's Spooktacular Fang-tastic Cast-iron Cauldron Cook-off, Miss Cindy Parker, with her Deliciously Decadent Devil's Food cake."

A roar greeted his lady, and she buried her face in her hands, as her competitors swamped her.

"All right, Russ." After taking hold of his son, Rafe slapped Russell on the back. "Go get her."

"We love you." George blew him a kiss.

"Good luck." Tony waved.

After weaving through the pack, Russ skipped up the side stairs. As arranged, once the announcer awarded the blue ribbon, Minnie gave Cindy a slim rectangular box. When his sweet baker lifted the lid, she snapped to attention and scanned the audience, no doubt, for him.

Homing in on her emotions, he sensed her desire, and everything centered on him and how she planned to celebrate their engagement. Of course, she answered him before he ever popped the question, but he'd do so, anyway, because he owed her that.

It was then he walked onto the stage, to

hoots and hollers from his cheering section, and she spotted him. Immediately, she burst into tears, just as he anticipated, because he knew a lot about his sentimental lady, about her capacity for understanding, forgiveness, and, above all, unconditional love.

And she'd taught him so much about who he was and the man he wanted to be, for her, for the family they would create, and for the memories they would make as they did everything—together.

From the box, he drew the heavily starched apron strings, untied the knot at one end, and freed the diamond engagement ring he'd secured there. Then he knelt, and the crowd went wild.

Holding her hand, he gazed into her beautiful blue eyes and smiled. "Cindy Parker, will you marry me?"

Nodding furiously, she cried, as he slipped the ring on her finger. Then he stood, lifted her into his arms, and twirled her about, as the audience erupted.

"Well, folks. I think she said yes," the emcee proclaimed. "Let's congratulate the happy couple."

Yes, he could have done something romantic and private, but she still suffered moments of uncertainty, given what happened so long ago, and he figured a proposal offered the perfect opportunity to bury the last remnants of that awful night, once and for all.

"Russell Lee, I'll love you till I die, and even then, I'm betting you'll still hold my heart," she whispered in his ear.

"Aw, baby, I love you, too." Shifting, he caressed her cheek with his thumb and kissed her. "And everyone knows that you're my girl, now and forever."

Cindy rubbed her nose to his. "Yes, they do."

ABOUT BARBARA DEVLIN

USA Today Bestselling, Amazon All-Star author Barbara Devlin was born a storyteller, but it was a weeklong vacation to Bethany Beach, DE that forever changed her life. The little house her parents rented had a collection of books by Kathleen Woodiwiss, which exposed Barbara to the world of romance, and Shanna remains a personal favorite. Barbara writes heartfelt historical romances that feature flawed heroes who may know how to seduce a woman but know nothing of marriage. And she prefers feisty but smart heroines who sometimes save the hero, before they find their happily ever after. Barbara earned an MA in English and continued a course of study for a Doctorate in Literature and Rhetoric. She happily considered herself an exceedingly eccentric English professor, until success in Indie publishing lured her into writing, full-time, featuring her fictional knighthood, the Brethren of the Coast.

Connect with Barbara Devlin at BarbaraDevlin.com, where you can sign up for her newsletter, The Knightly News.
Facebook:
https://www.facebook.com/BarbaraDevlinAuthor
Twitter: @barbara_devlin

TITLES BY BARBARA DEVLIN

BRETHREN OF THE COAST
Loving Lieutenant Douglas: A Brethren of the Coast
Novella
Enter the Brethren
My Lady, the Spy
The Most Unlikely Lady
One-Knight Stand
Captain of Her Heart
The Lucky One
Love with an Improper Stranger
To Catch a Fallen Spy
Hold Me, Thrill Me, Kiss Me: A Brethren of the Coast
Novella
The Duke Wears Nada
Owner of Lonely Heart (2018)

BRETHREN ORIGINS
Arucard
Demetrius
Aristide
Morgan

PIRATES OF THE COAST
The Black Morass
The Iron Corsair
The Buccaneer
The Marooner
Once Upon a Christmas Knight

KATHRYN LE VEQUE'S KINDLE WORLD OF DE
WOLFE PACK
Lone Wolfe
The Big Bad De Wolfe
Tall, Dark & De Wolfe (January 2018)